JAKE AR

SPARTANS OF TI

AND OTHER STORIES

SPARTANS OF THE CORRIB AND OTHER STORIES

Cover image: Tiramisu Studio/Shutterstock.com
Cover design and typesetting: Jake Arden

ISBN: 978-1508645078
ISBN-13: 978-1508645078

ABOUT THE AUTHOR

Jake Arden was born in Galway, Ireland. His playwright parents, John Arden and Margaretta D'Arcy, followed an unconventional lifestyle. Much of Jake's childhood was spent on a small island in Lough Corrib without running water, electricity or telephone. An overland trip to India by Land Rover in 1969 (with his mother driving) led to the whole family being gaoled in Assam for being Maoist spies. The consequences of his parents' political activism in the 1970s and 80s included the local branch of the Official IRA ordering Margaretta's assassination, her imprisonment in Armagh jail for taking non-violent direct action in support of the Republican hunger strikers and a costly libel action over one of their plays which lost them the island. Jake now lives quietly in Walthamstow with his wife Cathy.

To find out more about the author, visit **jakearden.com**

"Of all men's miseries the bitterest is this: to know so much and to have control over nothing."
Herodotus, Histories

CONTENTS

SPARTANS OF THE CORRIB

CHAPTER 1

THE CALM BEFORE THE STORM

Joe Hill was bored. He sat on the end of the pier looking out across the shimmering water of the lake to where his older brothers, Nathan and David, were fishing. The white, wooden, rowing boat was becalmed in the deep water channel that lay between the headland of Ford's farm and the rocky limestone shelf that extended from the island. The brothers were taking it in turns to stand up and cast out. Joe had wanted to go fishing as well, but Nathan had said no. "You don't how to fish properly. You rock the boat, you tangle up your line, you tangle up my line, you scare the fish, you're not coming." Joe hated Nathan. He hated David as well for siding with Nathan. He was beginning to hate being on the island.

Last summer had been much better. There had been lots of other people. The hippies had come and built a great bonfire. Everyone had stood round beating tom-toms, bashing tambourines, blowing whistles, making a fantastic noise. Joe and his brothers had danced round the huge flames, whooping like Red Indians, cheered on by the adults. Then the American couple had visited, Frank and Jill. Frank had a big moustache and a ponytail and he told them stories about the Spartans. How boys were trained to become warriors from the age of six. How the mother of a Spartan would hand him a shield on the eve of battle and tell him to come home alive with it or dead on it. And Joe and his brothers became Spartans and they had a brilliant running battle with swords, spears and shields in the rain along the shoreline. And then there was Jill, beautiful Jill with her long blonde hair. Sunbathing on her own at the top of the island. Sunbathing without a top on. With nipples the size of cherries.

But this year there had been no visitors. Mother and Father said they had work to do and couldn't be distracted. Nathan was now eleven and said that the games Joe liked playing were childish and David agreed with him. And that left only Daniel.

Joe went to find his younger brother. He walked up the shore, through the screen of hawthorn trees and gorse bushes into the clearing where the buildings stood. The largest was the White House, a flat-roofed wooden chalet that was raised above the ground on concrete stilts. This was where the family cooked and ate and where Joe, David and Daniel slept. Set apart from this was a much older, wooden shack with a rusty corrugated iron roof and a veranda. This was where Mother and Father slept and worked. Adjoining that was a six foot by six foot shed where Nathan slept so that he did not have to share a bedroom in the White House.

The ground around the buildings had been cultivated by Mother. Potatoes were growing at the front and lettuce and herbs at the back. At the side of the White House were clumps of rhubarb, some blackberry bushes and two apple trees between which was stretched a hammock. Daniel lay in the hammock looking at a picture book. Joe came up and pushed the hammock to make it swing.

"Stop it," said Daniel. "I'm reading."

"Liar," Joe said. "You're only looking at the pictures."

"I'm reading. Now go away."

"Reading's boring. Let's do something interesting. We could have a wrestle."

"I don't want a wrestle. I want to read."

"Do you want to come for a swim?"

"No."

"Stuff you then," said Joe.

He walked round the front of the White House to the Shack. The clatter of a typewriter came from inside.

"Mother, when are we going to eat?" he called through the open door.

"Not for a while yet," Mother said from inside. "Have some bread if you're hungry."

"Don't want bread", Joe said, kicking the side of the Shack.

The clatter of the typewriter keys stopped. "Stop that Joseph," his mother shouted. "I'm trying to work."

"Stuff you too," said Joe.

On the walls either side of the door, protected from the rain by the veranda, hung a selection of tools including a garden fork, a spade, a hoe, a band saw, a large axe and a hatchet. Joe took the hatchet down and walked up the path between the neatly tended salad beds. He walked past the concrete-covered cess pit and its sickly stench into the woods. It was dark and cooler here. Moss covered rocks marked the boundaries of old potato fields. Father had said that once the whole island would have been cultivated but that the Great Potato Famine had ended that. He came to a big birch tree with low hanging branches and hacked off the straightest looking bough with the hatchet. He then spent a few minutes stripping away the bark and cutting a point. Sticking the hatchet into the waistband of his shorts, he held his spear in front of him and advanced deeper in the thicket. A rustling sound came from a bramble bush to his right. He stopped. He hoped it was a bird but then started to worry that it might be a rat. He had come across the corpse of a rat in these woods before. It had lain on the pathway, big and bloated, belly up with congealed blood around its mouth and its large teeth bared. He shuddered at the memory and hurried on along the path until the darkness gave way again to bright sunlight and he emerged on the east side of the island.

The shoreline of this side was studded with slabs of flat limestone which were pitted with holes and contained fossils of snails. Hopscotching his way across the slabs Joe made his way north until he came to a grove of tall sycamore trees. In a glade in the grove a shabby, grey canvas tent was pitched: Father's workspace. The sound of singing was coming from inside.

"Said the lord unto his lady as he rode over the moss
Beware of Long Lankin that lives amongst the gorse
Beware the moss, beware the moor, beware of Long Lankin
Be sure the doors are bolted well
Lest Lankin should creep in."

He stood at the edge of the glade puzzled. Father said that he had to go to the tent to write. So that he could get some peace and quiet.

So why was he singing? And why was he singing about Long Lankin?

"We will pinch him, we will prick him, we will stab him with a pin

And the nurse shall hold the basin for the blood all to run in

So they pinched him, then they pricked him, then they stabbed him with a pin

And the false nurse held the basin for the blood all to run in."

Joe thought about going over and opening the flap of the tent. But then he thought, what if Long Lankin was in the tent with Father? What if it wasn't Father singing, but Long Lankin?

"There was blood all in the kitchen

There was blood all in the hall

There was blood all in the parlour

Where my lady she did fall."

"Father?" Joe called.

The singing stopped.

"Father? Is that you?" He drew the hatchet from his waistband.

The flap of the tent was pulled back and the head of Father poked out.

"Who's there?" Father said.

"It's me," Joe said.

Father looked at Joe through his thick-rimmed black spectacles.

"Is supper ready?"

"No. I just thought I would visit you."

"I'm working Joe. We can talk over supper."

"When is that going to be?"

Father stuck his arm through the flap and peered at his watch. "It's four o'clock now, so it will be in two hours."

"But I'm starving. I can't wait that long."

"Your mother made some bread this morning, why don't you go back to the house and eat that."

"I don't want to eat her bread."

"I haven't got any food here, so I can't help you. Now please leave me alone." Father drew his head back into the tent.

Joe considered severing the guy ropes of the tent with his hatchet, but thought better of it. He walked out of the glade as Father resumed the ballad.

"Now Long Lankin shall be hanged
From the gallows oh so high
And the false nurse shall be burned
In the fire close by."

CHAPTER 2

LOAVES AND FISHES

David was rowing and Nathan sat in the stern shouting directions. Navigating the boat into its berth along a dredged channel between two dry-stoned piers was tricky. You needed to keep a straight line. Too far to port and you risked scraping the bow against a series of jagged submerged rocks; too far to starboard and you could run aground on a shingle bank. David's line was good. He pulled a final stroke and slid the oars out of the rowlocks to rest on the gunnels as the boat flowed in, its keel crunching on the shingle beneath. The boys scrambled out of the boat and dragged its bow out of the water. As Nathan secured its bow line with a reef knot to a ring set in a heavy piece of concrete, David retrieved the rods, fishing tackle and a bucket from the boat.

"Did you catch anything?" Joe shouted.

Nathan was scowling but David was beaming. "A pike."

"It's not still alive is it?" Joe said.

"No we killed it, but it was a hell of a job," David said.

"You mean I killed it," said Nathan.

"Yeah, Nathan had to kill it. It was flapping all over the boat trying to bite us but he whacked it on the head with a rowlock," said David.

"You were shitting yourself," said Nathan.

"No I wasn't. I removed the hook, didn't I?"

"Let's see?" said Joe.

As David tilted the bucket for Joe to see, Nathan suddenly reached in and pulled the pike out. He squeezed its green-black neck and its jaws opened, baring rows of razor sharp teeth which he thrust towards Joe's face.

Joe screamed and stumbled back. "Get it away!"

Nathan laughed. "It's evil looking isn't it," he said, before dropping the pike back in the bucket and wiping the slime from his hand on his trousers.

"I couldn't believe it when it took my spinner," David said. "My rod bent over double and when I was reeling it in it looked like a monster."

"It's only a baby," Nathan said dismissively. "Not even three pounds. The one I hooked was much bigger."

"So where's your one then?" said Joe regaining his composure.

"It was so big the line broke."

"But your rod didn't move, Nathan," David said. "All you did was snag a rock."

"Shut up. It was a massive pike right. I saw it."

"If you say so," said David.

Mother was tending to two blackened pots bubbling on the gas cooker when they entered the White House. Daniel stood next to their mother mixing something in a large cake bowl. The gate-leg table had been extended and was clear except for a large and uncut home-made loaf of soda bread.

"What's for dinner?" asked Nathan.

"Tuna fish surprise," said Mother without turning round. "And Daniel's making us a nice dessert."

Nathan went to inspect the contents of Daniel's bowl. "What is that, it looks like shite?"

"It's not shite, its chocolate covered cornflakes," said Daniel.

"But we don't have any chocolate," said Joe.

"It's cocoa," said Daniel offering a dollop on his finger. "Do you want to taste."

"No," said Joe.

David had made his way to the stainless-steel sink with his bucket.

"What are you doing?" Nathan said.

"I'm going to fry my pike," David said.

"Not now, David," Mother said. "I'm making you a lovely dinner, why don't you cook it tomorrow?"

"I don't want tuna fish surprise. I'm fed up with tuna fish surprise. It's disgusting and we have it every week so how can it be a surprise. I want my pike," said David.

"You heard what Mother said," Nathan said. "You're not cooking that pike."

Nathan grabbed the bucket. David grabbed it back and there was a struggle which ended when Nathan poked David in the eye with his finger and David fled crying out of the house.

"Nathan," Mother said. "You shouldn't poke David in the eye, it's dangerous. Now go after him and apologise."

"He started it," said Nathan.

"I don't care who started it, just do what I say."

"Now Joseph, you can help me by laying the table." Mother said.

"Okie, dokie,"he said, bending down to open the cupboard where the crockery was kept. "But there's no plates."

"They must all be in the washing up tub. Be a dear and wash some for me. There's hot water in the kettle."

"Do I have to?"

"Yes you do or you don't eat."

Daniel started laughing.

"Great," said Joe.

Joe went out the front door and down the concrete blocks which served as steps. The washing-up tub stood by the steps. It was a tin bath full to the brim with cold water with a greasy green film on the surface. Joe reached into the slimy water, grimacing, and retrieved six plates with a red-checked pattern and six forks. He shook the water off them and took them back inside to the sink, which he filled with warm water from a large battered kettle taken from the hob of the gas cooker. He added some washing up liquid and washed the grease off the plates and forks then dried them with a soiled tea towel. He then set the table.

Daniel had moulded his mix into little cakes which he set in a baking tray. He showed them proudly to Mother.

"They look lovely dear. I'll put them in the oven for you," Mother said, taking the tray.

Daniel joined Joe at the table and they both sat down on stools and held their forks expectantly.

"I'm so hungry I could eat a horse," said Joe.

"I could eat a heffalump," said Daniel.

As Mother set the pots from the cooker on the table. David and Nathan entered. David's face was streaked with tears and he sat down at the table without speaking. Nathan was smiling.

A booming voice was heard from outside. "Fee, fie, foe, thumb, I smell the blood of...." Father entered, stopped by the table and sniffed. "Hmm, now what is that I smell?

"Tuna fish surprise!" shouted Daniel.

"Yum, yum. Just what a giant needs after a hard day's gianting," Father said, sitting down at the table with a big grin.

Mother began serving. Plates were passed to her and ladled with a mound of white sticky rice and a slop of a grey glutinous sauce before being passed back.

"Now does anyone want a nice slice of bread?" she said, taking a knife to the slab of soda bread.

The brothers, mouths full of food looked at each other and smiled, even David managed to raise a smile.

"I'll have a slice. It looks yummy," Father said.

Mother began cutting the bread. The knife made a rasping sound as it sawed through the thick knobbled crust.

"Are you sure that's not concrete?" Joe asked.

"No, no, it's just got a fine crust," she said, pressing down on the knife.

As she cleaved through the bottom crust to produce the first slice, the loaf suddenly flipped off the table and landed with a thud on the floor.

Daniel's mouth exploded in laughter, spewing out bits of rice. The other brothers joined in. Even Father chuckled. But Mother was not amused. She bent down, picked up the loaf and slammed in on the table, rattling the plates.

"I've had it with you lot of you," she screamed. "I'm slaving over a hot stove, day in day out, and this is the gratitude I get."

"Now, now Rebecca," Father said. "There's no harm done."

"Yes there is. And you're the worst Jeffery. You spend all day in your tent leaving me to look after these ungrateful brats and then you think you can laugh at me. Well you can't." She stormed out of the house.

Father looked around the table sheepishly and then stood up. "Boys, you really should try to show your mother some respect," he said following Mother out of the door.

The brothers sat in silence for a minute, then Joe started to laugh. He abruptly stopped when Nathan delivered a vicious kick to his shin under the table.

"Now look what you've done," Nathan said.

"Owwh, that hurt, I didn't do anything," Joe said, rubbing his shin.

David suddenly sniffed the air. "Can anyone smell burning?"

"My chocolate cornflakes!" Daniel shouted and ran over to the oven. He pulled the door open and reached inside for the tray. As he tried to pull it out, he screamed and dropped the tray spilling black lumps across the floor. He looked at the burnt cakes and then at his hand and then started bawling.

"Shut up you big baby," said Nathan. He went over to Daniel, grabbed his hand and inspected it. "It's not even burnt," he said. Daniel stopped crying. Nathan turned to Joe. "Clear up the mess," he ordered.

"Why me?"

"Because I said so. And you David can clear the table."

Joe picked up the burnt cakes from the floor. He took a nibble of one. It tasted like charcoal. He chucked the cakes in the steel dustbin which stood by the cooker. He felt terribly hungry.

"I'm going to get an orange," he said to his brothers.

"Well bring back one for all of us then," said Nathan. "Don't be selfish."

CHAPTER 3

THE GREAT HUNGER

Joe's parents kept the crate of oranges in the Shack so they could be guarded and rationed. They were the main source of fresh fruit for Joe and his brothers until the blackcurrants, blackberries and later the apples ripened in the garden. Or until the family made a shopping expedition to the village on the mainland.

As Joe approached the hut he could hear Mother and Father arguing.

"No Jeffrey, it's simply not fair leaving me with the children all day. You're not the only bloody writer on this island. I need time to work as well."

"But Rebecca…"

"No buts Jeffrey. I will have my way."

The door was open and Father was sitting at the table on which was set a typewriter and a pile of papers and books. He had his head down and was polishing his glasses on his crumpled shirt. Mother was standing over him. Hands on hips, her eyes flashing. She looked at Joe coldly as he came to the doorway.

"What do you want?"

"Can I have an orange?"

She shook her head. "I don't think there are any left Joseph."

"There must be."

She bent down beside the table and picked up the wooden slatted crate with Jaffa printed on the sides. She held it open to Joe and shook it. "See for yourself."

Joe shoved his hands into the crate and rummaged through a jumble of blue tissue-paper squares. There were no oranges. He felt tears coming to his eyes.

"I so wanted an orange."

"Well you'll have to wait until we go to the village."

"When's that going to be?"

"Soon."

"Can we go tomorrow?"

"We will go to the village when I'm ready to go to the village. Now leave us."

"It's not fair."

"No, it's not fair is it Jeffrey?"

Father held his hands up. "Oh please Rebecca."

Joe turned from them with hot tears beginning to trickle down his cheek. He went down the lake shore and walked to the end of the pier where he sat with his legs dangling over the water and buried his head in his hands. He let himself cry, allowing great sobs to bubble up and break into his palms and the tears and snot to flow. And as he cried he rocked himself gently. Then after a while he stopped. He wiped the mucus from his hands on his shorts and cleared his eyes.

The waters of the lake were absolutely calm and like the flat surface of a mirror. The sky was clear blue and the rays of the sun, which was balanced over the dark mountains of Connemara to the south west, sprinkled the water with shards of gold.

Joe imagined the rowing boat cutting through the water on its way to the mainland, the oars pulled by his father slicing cleanly into the surface, creating little whirlpools as he pulled back. And then the squeak on the rowlocks as the oars were jerked out with the drips from them creating circles on each side of the wake behind the boat.

Next he imagined all of them piling into the mud-splattered, battered blue Land Rover parked by the ghillie's hut on the landing area. Mother, tiny behind the big steering wheel, the engine roaring into life. Bumping over the potholes on the unpaved track leading from the lake and brushing against bramble bushes until they reached tarmac.

Then arriving in the village, following the trail of brown cow splats on the main road. Parking outside Keogh's general store. Farmers trading cattle at the crossroads in the front of the Anglers' Hotel. Spitting on their palms before shaking hands to do the deal. Small boys in dung-encrusted wellington boots, keeping the cows in line with sticks. Fisherman coming out of Tucks, laden with rods and tackle, heading down to the lake to catch trout.

Loading up the boxes of supplies into the back of the Land Rover: a crate of oranges, a box of dark green shiny Granny Smiths, bunches of bananas, fresh milk, fresh eggs, fresh soft white bread, fresh sausages and bacon, everything smelling fresh. A big wedge of cheddar cheese wrapped in greaseproof paper, its cheesy aroma permeating everywhere, getting the juices in the mouth and the tummy flowing. A huge slab of thick cooking chocolate.

The scramble into the sweet shop. Blowing all their pocket money on selections from the big glass jars on the shelves behind the counter. Little paper bags filled with pear drops, bull eyes, gob stoppers and toffees.

They had to go to the village tomorrow, he decided. Mother couldn't let them starve to death. That is how it felt like. The hole inside of him was so huge, he must be starving. His stomach was so empty it hurt. He leant out over the pier and scooped up a cupped handful of water. He sucked it into his mouth. It was warm and sweet, but not in a nice way. He knew that even if he drank the whole lake it would not fill the hole. He spat the water out. And then he thought, of course he wasn't starving. The people who died in the famine were starving. They were so hungry they had to eat grass and when they found their bodies there was green juice dribbling down their chins. There was food he could eat, if he really wanted to. He could go inside and eat a slice of Mother's bread. That would fill him up. Or he could make a bowl of cornflakes with diluted condensed milk and sugar poured over it. But he didn't want to.

No he decided, it was better to feel like this. Being hungry would not have bothered the Spartans. They could go for days without food and still fight and win a battle. They were hard and lean and tough. They had to be tough. If a baby was weak it was left out on the mountains to die. The Spartan who ran the marathon was the toughest of the tough. He hadn't eaten for days. He had fought with 300 Spartans at the pass of Monopoly holding off thousands of Persians and then had run hundreds of miles in his bare feet to bring reinforcements.

CHAPTER 4

THE STORM

Joe heard the crunch of footsteps behind him. He turned. It was Daniel.

"What are you doing?" said Daniel.

"Just sitting," said Joe.

"Nathan sent me to find you. He wants to know where the oranges are."

"They're all gone."

"Oh," said Daniel. "I've got a blister on my hand do you want to see it?"

"No", said Joe. Daniel turned away and Joe suddenly felt sorry. "Go on then. Let me see."

Daniel came over and held out his hand. Joe looked at the blister. It was the size of a sixpence. "Does it hurt?"

"It did at first, but not now," said Daniel, sitting down beside Joe.

"Good man. Spartans don't feel pain."

"Am I a Spartan?"

"Yes."

"Why?"

"Because I'm a Spartan and you're my brother. That makes you a Spartan. If you'd been weak you'd have been left out to die."

"Was Alfred the Great a Spartan?"

"No. Why?"

"Because David said Alfred the Great burnt his cakes as well and that's what made him great."

Joe laughed. Daniel laughed as well. "What's so funny?"

"You are," said Joe.

Daniel laughed again and then suddenly stopped.

"What's that over there?" he said pointing out across the lake.

Joe looked. At the north end of the lake a bank of black clouds was building.

"Do you think it's a fire?" Daniel said.

"I don't know," said Joe. "It doesn't look like a fire."

He stood up and put a finger in his mouth. Whetting it with spit, he held it up in front of him. The waters of the lake were still calm but he felt a very subtle cool whisper of a breeze on his finger. The height of the black clouds was increasing.

"The weather's changing."

Ripples began spreading down the lake. He could now feel the breeze on his cheeks. It was gaining in strength. The ripples beyond Ford's headland were turning into waves. Now the wind was really gusting. Joe spread out his arms and let his body absorb the warm force of it. Water began lapping at the end of the pier. At the far end of the lake he could see white crests appearing. Sea horses, driving in wedges down the exposed stretch of water towards the island.

"A storm!" he shouted to Daniel. "We're going to be hit by a storm."

He felt a charge of excitement flood through him. Now he could feel flecks of warm water stinging into his cheeks. Rain was peppering the strengthening waves.

"We should go in," said Daniel.

"No. Do you remember the storm last summer. When Jill and Frank were here?"

"Yeah"

"Do you remember we all went out in the middle of it. Stripped to the waist. Pretended we were Spartans."

"Yeah."

"Well wasn't it fantastic? Come on, let's do it again."

He punched his fist in the air. "Spartans to battle!"

Daniel looked at Joe and then stood up and turned his face into the wind. He smiled and then punched his fist into the air. "Alfred the Great to battle!"

"Come on let's get the others. Last one to the house is a Persian," Joe said breaking into a sprint.

"That's not fair," shouted Daniel behind him. "I wasn't ready."

With the wind behind him Joe flew up the shore and zig-zagged through the screen of trees.

16

"Spartans to arms!"

David came to the door of the White House. "What's going on?"

"It's a storm. We're going to have a battle. Like we did last year. Come on."

David smiled. "Okay, but we need armour."

Daniel came up puffing and the three of them bundled up the steps into the living room. Nathan was sitting at the table painting an Airfix model of a Stuka.

"What's going on?" Nathan said.

"We're going to have a battle," said Joe. "Spartans versus the Persian storm. You can be a Spartan if you like."

"I'm not being anything. It's stupid," Nathan said.

David took the large metal lid from the rubbish dustbin and grabbed a tin colander from the draining board of the sink which he put on his head. Daniel meanwhile had been in his bedroom and emerged with a plastic Roman breastplate, sword and helmet. Joe in turn took the lid from a second metal bin which was used to store sugar, flour, rice and cereal to protect it from the rats, and the large cooking pot which fitted his head nicely but was rather heavy.

"I need a shield," said Daniel.

Joe gave him the lid of the cooking pot. "Have that."

"It's too small."

"No it's not. You've got your breastplate."

"I'm going to give you all three seconds to get out of here before I start punching you," Nathan said. "One…."

"Come on!" said David. And they all scrambled to the door.

"Two…"

David was first out. Daniel was next but he hesitated and Joe had to push him down the steps. He closed the door behind him shutting out Nathan as he said three.

The wind was howling through the trees around the house. As Daniel struggled into his breastplate, Joe searched for and found his birch spear and David pulled an old broom handle out from under the house. With Daniel leading the way, his plastic sword pointed forward, they ran down the path.

On the exposed foreshore they ran into a wall of wind, spume and rain which forced them back on their heels and lifted Daniel's helmet from his head and sent it sailing back into the trees.

"Form a phalanx!" David shouted, taking command.

Joe slapped down on the cooking pot to fix it firmly to his head and bent down behind his dustbin lid shield against the force of the wind. Holding his spear tightly in his armpit he closed with Daniel and locked arms with him. On other side, David performed a similar manouever until a tight sandwich was achieved with Daniel in the middle. Then with shields lifted, spears and swords front and heads down, they advanced on the lake.

Huge waves were now smashing into the pier and the stern of the rowing boat. The whole of the lake was in a violent commotion, the peaks of each wave exploding into raging white spray.

"Defend the pass of Monopoly!" Joe screamed, pulling the others forward to the pier and the breaking waves.

"Its Thermopolyae you idiot!" David roared. "Not Monopoly."

"Whatever," Joe retorted, laughing.

Bunching together even closer they pushed on along to the end of the pier. There they huddled, ankle deep in the wash from the breaking waves, screaming into the wind.

The rain was driving horizontally, stinging Joe's exposed flesh, rattling against the dustbin lid. He held his shield firm and his spear steady, imagining the rain as Persian arrows.

"We shall not retreat," he shouted. "Die wind, die!"

"Get back you Persian waves!" David shouted.

"Die waves, die!" Daniel joined in.

And then it seemed as the ferocity of the wind was weakening.

"We're winning," Joe yelled.

"It might be a trick, hold firm," said David.

"I'm getting very wet," said Daniel.

Suddenly something stabbed Joe in the back. He felt a sharp, stinging pain and screamed. He dropped his spear and shield and, clutching his hand to his spine to locate the injury, wheeled round.

Nathan stood at the shoreside end of the pier holding a metal catapult, a look of murderous hatred on his face. He drew up the catapult and stretched back the black rubber thong, aiming at Joe's face.

"Surrender or die!" Nathan shouted.

Joe's stomach sharply contracted. He felt sick. If Nathan released the catapult he was going to be seriously hurt.

David had now turned and Nathan switched his aim to David's face.

"Surrender now. All of you!" Nathan shouted again. With the catapult held taut in front of him, be began to advance, closing the range of his shot.

Daniel was cowering behind Joe. Joe looked for help to David. David looked towards Nathan, but not in terror. In his eyes was anger.

"Stop it!" David shouted. "Just stop it. This is our game and you said you didn't want to play."

"Surrender then," Nathan said.

"Why?" David demanded.

"Because you are Sparta and I am Rome and I have a catapult. Veni, Vidi, Vici." He was now only a few feet from David.

David did not flinch. "Fine," he said, dropping his dustbin and broom handle. "I surrender. But it doesn't mean anything because it's only a stupid game and I'm not playing any more."

"I'm not playing anymore," Nathan mimicked. He turned the catapult back to Joe. "Are you playing anymore Joe or are you going to surrender?"

Tears began to fill Joe's eyes. He didn't want to surrender but he also didn't want to be hurt. He wanted to kill Nathan, but his body had drained of strength.

"I don't want to play anymore either," said Daniel.

"So you surrender then?" Nathan asked Daniel, keeping the catapult on Joe.

"Yes," said Daniel. "But I'm keeping my sword".

"That's okay," said Nathan. "Rome allows those who surrender with honour to keep their arms. Now that just leaves you Joe. I'm going to count to three."

Joe desperately wished David would do something. But David just stood there with his arms folded glaring at Nathan.

"One…" Nathan counted.

Joe's strongest thought then was Spartans do not surrender. But this was only a game - he was not a Spartan.

"Two…." Nathan said. "I mean it Joe."

"Okay," said Joe "I surrender." But his words were drowned out by an enormous crack of thunder and for an instant Nathan and the whole island behind him was lit up with a brilliant white light.

Nathan started and released his hand from the thong of the catapult. "Jesus," he said, looking beyond Joe into the lake. "Did you see that?"

"We need to go in," said David. "This is dangerous."

He pushed past Nathan, with Daniel following.

Joe turned his eyes to the lake as a second thunder clap exploded around him. A fork of lightning shot through the black clouds and speared into the channel in front of Ford's headland. For a second the turmoil of the waves on the lake was frozen as if in a photograph.

"Get inside!" Nathan shouted.

Joe started to run. Nathan was ahead of him sprinting, catching up on David and Daniel who had almost reached the tree line.

They bunched up as they approached the white house. Running out to meet them was Mother, her long black hair flying out in the wind. She was screaming. "Get inside, get inside!"

CHAPTER 5

ONCE A SPARTAN ALWAYS A SPARTAN

Mother dried Daniel's hair with a towel. "You should never, ever, ever be in exposed place when lightening strikes."

"You should listen to your mother," Father said. "That's how your great uncle Charles was killed." He handed round a selection of ragged towels to Nathan, Joe and David.

"I thought he fell off a mountain," said David.

"No that was great uncle Albert. Charles was killed while playing golf," Father said.

"I thought you had more sense, Nathan," Mother said. "You are meant to look after your younger brothers."

"But that's what I was doing," said Nathan glaring at David and Joe. "I told them to come in."

"That's not true," came a muffled protest from Daniel.

"Anyhow, you're all safe now," Mother said. "The lightning will hit the trees before it hits the house."

Father went round the room lighting candles. The room glowed yellow. Outside it was completely black.

"Will you be sleeping in here tonight, Nathan?" Father asked.

"No, I'm not scared of a little lightning. I'll be fine in my shed," Nathan replied.

"Of course you will," Father said. "Now who wants a nice cup of cocoa?"

Joe lay in his bunk bed listening to the wind howl outside. He had not surrendered he told himself. The words had come out, but Nathan had not heard them, so they did not count. He was still a Spartan. He was the last to run from the lightning as well. That meant something too.

He leant over the edge of the bunk. "Daniel, are you asleep?"

"What?" Daniel said.

21

"I didn't surrender you know. You and David did, but I didn't."

"I didn't really surrender either. I was pretending and I kept my sword."

"Alfred the Great eh?"

"No, I'm Daniel the Great."

Joe laughed and heard Daniel chuckle in return. He rolled onto his back and closed his eyes.

THE INHALATION

The stink of the Liffey was rising as Joe turned off the quay into O'Connell Street. He stopped to check his Timex. It was hard to see the hands through the spidery cracks in the glass but he could make out that it was twenty five to three. Nathan had said to be outside the cinema at half past. Joe was late. Heading north up the wide thoroughfare, he zigzagged through crowds of shoppers until he reached the bookstall that was pitched on the pavement opposite the General Post Office.

He stopped and cast his eyes up and down the ranks of paperbacks, his pupils widening as he took in the images on the glossy covers. Mandingo, the stud of the plantation, standing proud, bare-chested with the fingers of the white slave-owner's daughter caressing his oiled black muscles. A space goddess, breasts spilling out of a skimpy silk dress, waiting to service the Synthetic Men of Mars. The blonde biker mama, red lips around a king-size cigarette, desperate for the Black Leather Barbarians to liberate her from her tight, shiny cat suit. Joe felt the urgent heat of a horn beginning to rise in his crotch. His eyes travelled further along the rack until they reached the Richard Allen collection: Skinhead, Farewell Skinhead, Skinhead Returns, illustrated by portraits of the hero in various aggressive poses.

Joe smiled at the thought that he shared the first name and initials. Joe Hawkins and Joe Hill. JH for aggro. Face staring right at you saying don't mess with me or you get a stomping. You gave Joe a problem and you got a boot in the bollocks.

Further down were two new books: Sorts, which featured some tough-looking teenage girls on the cover, and Smoothies, which had three long-haired youths in fancy suits. Joe turned the book over to read the blurb on the back and flicked through the pages. He handed the stall holder a fifty pence coin, received his change and slipped the paperback into the pocket of his denim jacket.

Moving away from the stall he stopped to admire his reflection in the big plate-glass windows of Clery's department store. Not quite a smoothie, he thought. His arms were getting too long for the denim jacket, which was also getting a bit tatty. The polyester star jumper and the draylon, six-button, high-waisted blue bags came from the January sales and they were both in reasonable condition. The blue-suede wedges had been bought in the summer sales and were getting very scuffed. But his 13th birthday was coming up and he would have to put some pressure on his mother for some new ones. But they had to be platforms. He hitched up his trousers so that his red socks were visible. He ran his fingers through his long blonde hair. It was greasy, but if he gave it a good wash and a blow dry it would be fine. He looked at his watch again. It was ten to three.

As he turned from the window he almost collided with a beggar woman who was advancing on him with her hand held out. Her other hand was clasped around a pink-faced baby who was swaddled to her waist by a tartan blanket. "Milk for the babby, for the love of Mary," she pleaded.

Joe recoiled. His nose wrinkled at the acrid smell of stale sweat and wood smoke, which wafted from the woman. He shook his head and side stepped her, but not before taking a look at her hand.

It's true, he thought. Travellers do not have any lines on their palms. He first had an inkling of this in the village school when he had made the mistake of calling Paddy Ward a knacker after Paddy had called him a pagan English fecker. Paddy had let Joe know how offensive he found the term by punching him on the nose and, as Joe tried to get in a counter blow, Brother Aloysius – the Bull – had stormed down the row, grabbed both of them by the ears and hauled them to the front of the class.

At this point Joe could have reminded the Bull that his mother had made it clear to the school that the Hill brothers were not allowed to suffer corporal punishment, in addition to being exempt from saying prayers, going to confession and preparing for confirmation. But he had chosen not to because he not want the word chicken-shite prefacing pagan English fecker on Paddy Ward's list of insults.

24

Joe had watched his adversary stretch out first one palm and then the other to receive the whistling stroke of the bamboo cane. Although impressed by the way Paddy took the punishment without flinching, he was more intrigued by the flat features of his palms. There was no heart- or life-line. But his thought were interrupted by the stinging shock delivered to his hand by the Bull's cane. For the second stroke he had to steel himself to avoid shaking or crying out, but he managed it. He then walked calmly back to his desk, sat down and reached under the desk to clasp the cool, soothing metal of its legs.

A queue was building up outside the Savoy cinema when he reached it. No sign of Nathan, but his younger brother, Daniel, was there. On his own. Wearing a parka with the hood up and looking worried. Joe came over and karate-chopped him lightly on the shoulder. "Watch out here comes the Big Boss, ha!" he said, smiling.

"Where you been? Nathan's going to kill you," Daniel said.

"Where is Nathan?"

"Gone looking for you. I don't understand why you couldn't have come with us. "

"Because I like being on my own and I wanted to buy a book. Have a dekko." He showed it to Daniel.

Daniel looked at the cover: "Smoothies? They look like spazzas."

"Better than the Moomen Troll crap you read Danbob. This is for big boys."

"I don't read Moomen Troll anymore, and stop calling me Danbob. Nathan's going to go mental if we don't join the queue."

Joe looked at the people gathering. Three girls, arm in arm, came clip clopping past in high wedges and wheeled in to form the end of the queue. Joe watched them as they chatted and laughed. They were older than Joe, fifteen, maybe even sixteen. He loved the sound of their Dublin accents. Not as good as a London accent, but better than the way the culchies out west talked. He also found the way their black maxi skirts curved tightly around their buttocks before flaring out in pleats very horny, as was the faint but musky scent of their perfume. He couldn't see their breasts from this angle but he could imagine the flesh bulging and straining in the soft white brassieres under their blouses. Much sexier than the girls in the village who smelt of milk on the turn and talcum powder and, who even when they were dressed up for Sunday mass, still looked old fashioned. Gurrier girls, he thought. Joe Hawkins would know how to give them a seeing too.

"Let's join the queue," Joe said. He positioned himself behind the girls, leaning back against the wall of the cinema in the pose of his hero, hands in the pockets of his jacket and one leg crossed over his knee.

"You've got holes in your socks," Daniel said. "You look like a divvy."

"What do you know." Joe said, sharply bringing his foot down to the ground.

Daniel rummaged in his pockets and produced a yellow block of sweets. "Do you want an Opal Fruit?"

"No. I'm going to have a smoke."

He turned to the wall to shield himself from the gaze of the girls and slipped his hands down the waistband of his trousers, into his underpants, from where he retrieved a crumpled blue ten-packet of Richmond. He turned back and stuck a cigarette between his lips. Then using his left hand he fished a box of matches from his jacket pocket and with his thumb and forefinger pushed open the box, withdrew a match and manoeuvred it to strike against the abrasive edge. The match lit and he quickly drew it up to the tip of the cigarette. He squinted to see if any of the girls were watching him perform his trick. They were not.

He drew the flame of the match onto the cigarette tip until it glowed then blew out the match with exhaled smoke. He took a long pull, held the smoke in his mouth and released it very slowly through his nose. "Ah, that's good," he said.

"Can I have a drag?" said Daniel.

"No. You're eating an Opal Fruit. You'll bum suck it."

Daniel swallowed the sweet and smacked his lips to dry them out. "I won't. I promise."

"Okay. But only a lug."

"What's the difference between a lug and a drag?"

"A lug is one puff and a drag is three lugs. You can have a lug."

Daniel took the cigarette and puffed on it. He also held the smoke in his mouth but then pursed his lips and blew it out as a jumbled cloud.

26

"What are you trying to do?" Joe said.

"Make smoke rings."

"Here, let me show you."

Joe took the cigarette back and sucked it deeply. He centred his tongue in the middle of the smoke and began sharply forcing out rings of smoke. He looked again at the girls but they still had not noticed him.

"Do you think the fillim will be as good as Towering Inferno?" Daniel asked.

"Fillim," Joe mimicked. "You're talking like a culchie."

"No I'm not. I said film."

Joe laughed. "Of course you did. It's meant to be better. They got this thing called Sensorsurround so that when the earthquake happens the whole cinema shakes. You'll shit your pants."

"No I won't. You're the one who gets scared. You put a cushion over your face during that film about the screaming woman on telly."

"No I didn't."

"Yes you did."

"Shut it or I'll kung-fu you."

He took another pull of the cigarette and savoured the smoke in his mouth.

"Where the fuck have you been?" It was Nathan.

Joe shot a stream of smoke out of the side of his mouth, balled his fingers around the cigarette and slipped his cupped hand into his jacket pocket.

Nathan was sixteen, and although not much taller than Joe, was a lot better built. His hair was dark and cut short and he was wearing a blue Crombie overcoat with the red silk lining of the breast pocket pulled up into a handkerchief-shaped triangle. Nathan worked part time in the warehouse at Dunn's stores and did not have rely on their mother for money for clothes. Joe noticed that the girls were now showing an interest.

"I had things to do," Joe said.

"What things? I told you to meet us here at half past."

"I don't need to tell you my business. I was only a few minutes late."

"Don't back-chat me you little gobshite." Nathan's fist hovered in front of Joe's face.

Joe weighed up which would be a worse humiliation. Being seen to back down by the girls or being seen to be hit. "Look I'm sorry right. I wanted to buy a book."

"Show me."

"It's in my pocket." Joe made a fumbling attempt to pull the book out with his free hand but was conscious that smoke was wisping out of the other pocket and the heat of the tip of the cigarette was increasing.

Nathan's saw the smoke. He smiled. "Looks like you're on fire. Let me help."

He grabbed Joe's hand inside the pocket and crushed it. The hot ash burned into Joe's palm and he had to suppress a scream. He pulled his hand out, flicked away the glowing embers of tobacco and began frantically blowing on his palm to kill the pain.

Nathan laughed. "Oh dear. You're hurt. Let me put something on it."

He grabbed Joe's fingers and flattened out his hand. He then hawked up a wad of phlegm and spat it onto the burn. "That should do the trick."

Joe wrenched away his hand and rubbed the spit off on his sleeve. He felt tears filling his eyes. The girls had turned away in disgust.

"Looks like you're going to cry, Joe. Go on why don't you have a nice cry."

"Fuck off!" Joe said turning away. Daniel was staring at him with frightened eyes.

"No, I'm not going to fuck off," Nathan said, grabbing Joe's collar and swinging him slowly round. He pulled Joe's face close to his forehead.

"Give me the cigarettes," he said softly.

Joe tensed his neck in anticipation of the head butt. He stared into Nathan's eyes and felt the coldness of his hatred for his brother flood his body. A numbness replaced his fear, a numbness that would allow him to take the pain of Nathan's violence. His eyes were dry now. Dry and dead.

"Just give me the cigarettes Joe. You can make it easy for yourself or you can have it hard."

"Give him the cigarettes, Joe." The tremble in Daniel's voice collapsed Joe's defensive wall.

"Okay," he said. But it was not okay, he thought. He was stupid. He

28

should have kept a better look out and seen Nathan coming.

Nathan relaxed his grip and allowed Joe to reach into his trouser pocket and hand over the packet. Nathan took a cigarette out and produced a black Zippo lighter. He flipped the lid and struck the flint with one movement of his thumb. He lit up, inhaled and then blew his exhalation into Joe's face. He smiled and offered the packet to Joe. "You have one."

Joe hesitated. Nathan's smile was evil.

"Go on."

Joe reached in and pulled a cigarette out.

"Can I have one?" said Daniel.

"No you can't." said Nathan. "You're not old enough. But Joe is, aren't you Joe? Joe thinks he's the big man. Can't walk to the cinema with us. He's got to do things his way, even though I'm the one holding the money for him to see the film. Let me light you." Nathan held the Zippo out.

Joe smoothed his hair back from his forehead and gingerly bent down to the flame. Nathan allowed Joe to light and then snapped the lighter shut. Joe took a puff, held the smoke in his mouth and released it slowly through his nose.

Nathan smiled. "Is that what you call smoking?"

"Yeah," Joe said, feeling his cheeks beginning to burn with embarrassment.

"Show me again."

Joe pulled deeper on the cigarette and used his tongue to corral the smoke at the back of his mouth. He felt the urge to cough. Nathan's eyes were boring into him.

"See Joe what you're doing is not smoking. It's pretending."

Joe saw Nathan clench his fist and automatically tightened his stomach muscles. The action triggered a cough and he spluttered out the smoke.

"It's very simple, Joe. If you want to smoke you inhale. But I think you're too much of a baby to inhale."

"No I'm not."

"Well let's see you do it then."

Joe looked at Daniel. Daniel's face was expressionless. If he

29

retreated, he would lose Daniel's respect. But Nathan was right, his smoking was all about pretending. A careful pretence nurtured over the years from that first fumbling attempt in the toilet when he was six. He was scared of what would happen if he drew the smoke down into his lungs. But Nathan did it and his mother and father did it and millions of other people did it and nothing terrible happened to them.

He drew again on the cigarette but this time lightly. He then relaxed his chest and breathed from his belly allowing the smoke to be drawn into his lungs. There was an immediate reaction. He felt a rush to his head. He held the smoke in his lungs and the feeling of light-headedness increased. He exhaled. A warm sensation coursed through his body, then quickly receded. He took another pull. Again he felt slightly dizzy, but not nauseous. It was like being tipsy on alcohol, but for a much a shorter period. The tingle in the veins also reminded him of the exquisite outcome of masturbation, but again on a much smaller scale. He let the smoke drift out from his lungs.

It was easy, he thought. Nothing to be frightened of, in fact it could become a source of strength. Welcome to Hill country. The smooth taste of Joe Hill. You're never alone with a Richmond. It was all part of growing up. Fuck you Nathan. Soon, sooner than you think, my time will come.

"Can I have my cigarettes back now?" he asked.

Nathan looked at him and his smile had gone. "It still doesn't make you a man." He crushed the cigarette packet in his fist and handed it back. "In future you don't hide your cigarettes from me. Understand. And if I say we're meeting at two thirty. You're here at two thirty, understand."

"I understand," Joe said, looking Nathan in the eyes.

"Can I have a lug now?" Daniel asked. "I want to inhale as well."

"No you fucking can't," said Nathan. "Now come, on the queue's moving."

Daniel's face dropped, but as they shuffled towards the doors of the cinema, Joe whispered to his brother: "Sit next to me and wait till the lights go off, then you can. Now give us an Opal Fruit."

THE GOOD SON

The Ward men were outside the hospital just as Joe's mother had said they would be. Standing guard, dressed in leather jackets, jeans and trainers; giving each man approaching the main entrance the once over, checking that they were not a McDonagh on a mission to finish the job they had started outside the cathedral. They cast a critical eye over Joe but he got no sense of hostility. He in return subtly appraised their heavy, drink-reddened faces, wondering if Paddy Ward, the traveller boy with whom he had shared the pain of a caning at the village school two decades ago, was among them.

His mother had filled Joe in with the background to the drama soon after his arrival on the coach from Dublin. It was all about control of the drugs trade, she had said. The McDonaghs were trying to establish a monopoly of the trade and had used money to secure the subservience of most of the traveller families in Connaught and Munster. But the Wards had refused to be bought off and the McDonaghs had turned to violence. They had laid down a marker at the funeral of a Ward patriach in Tuam when they had attacked the mourners at the grave side and the fight had spread throughout the small market town until the Gardai had bought it under control. Fifteen Wards and seven McDonaghs were hospitalised.

The McDonaghs had pressed their advantage. Peadar "Mad Dog" McDonagh had challenged Malky Ward, the top man in the clan, to a one-on-one set to. The men from the two families had gathered in the car park of the cathedral and had formed a circle. The McDonaghs outnumbered the Wards by two to one but Malky, still holding to the travellers code, had hoped that his strength and courage and the speed of his fists would end the conflict in a time-honoured way. But Mad Dog had no intention of fighting a fair fight and, as Malky had advanced into the circle to go head to head, the other McDonaghs had whipped out slash hooks from under their jackets and ripped into the Wards.

31

Now Malky and eight of his kinfolk were in the Galway Regional Hospital and the remaining men were standing guard waiting for the next attack. Behind them, inside the doors of the hospital, were the Ward women, the last line of defence. In contrast to the menacing silence of their husbands and brothers, the women were talking loudly, but under the chatter Joe could sense their terrible fear.

The last thing his father needed was for a riot to break out in the hospital, he thought. It would finish him off.

He asked a nurse for directions to the High Dependency Unit and she pointed him down a corridor. As he walked the polished floor he looked around, trying to remember how the hospital had been the last time he was here, twenty-one years ago. This part was unfamiliar. He had been on wing, several floors up and had been able to see the cathedral from the windows of the ward. There was something different about the nurses as well. None of them were wearing the habit of a Sister. The nuns had flown the hospital.

The glass panels of a door to a darkened room gave him the opportunity to check his reflection. The black four-button suit had held its shape well during his journey. His girlfriend, Elisha had questioned his outfit when he had set off, saying that he looked like he was going to a funeral, but he had argued that it was more important that he wore what he felt comfortable in. But now he questioned the wisdom of the black polo-neck jumper. He could feel sweat trickling down his back and beads of water were forming on his forehead. He felt very alone and wished Elisha was with him. He took a deep breath, dabbed his forehead with a tissue and walked on.

He gave the name of his father to a plump, rosy-cheeked young nurse sitting behind a desk guarding the doors of the HDU and she made a call on her telephone. Another fresh-faced nurse came out smiling and took Joe into the Unit. He was expecting bright clinical whiteness and lots of shiny steel and the smell of disinfectant. But instead the lights were dull, the walls were yellow and there was a lot of old, worn, wooden furniture and a smell of piss. He wondered if Malky or any of his brethen were in here and the scene from Godfather where Al Pacino wheels the bed and the drip of the critically bullet-wounded Marlon Brando to a safe room flashed through his mind.

They reached the bed of his father.

"Mr Hill, your son is here to see you, so he is. Isn't that a nice surprise now," the nurse said.

"He's doing grand but he gets tired very quickly," she said to Joe before leaving.

His father lay in a tangle of white sheets. He had tubes going into his nose and a drip in his arm. He looked pale and fragile. His mane of silver hair was unkempt and his chin was bristly with three day's growth. He turned his tired eyes to Joe and smiled weakly.

"Hiya Dad," Joe said softly. "How are you doing?"

He sat down on the bedside chair.

"I'm okay," his father wheezed. But he didn't look okay. Joe looked up to the heart monitor above the bed and tried to make out the significance of the green zig zags.

"I came as soon as I could."

Joe thought about reaching out to touch his father's hand. To show him he cared. But it did not seem right.

"The nurses seem nice, are they looking you after you?"

He had wanted to say so much. He had rehearsed it in his mind on the flight from London and on the coach. To tell his father that he loved him and did not want him to die. But none of it now seemed appropriate. He reached out and gently squeezed his father's hand.

"I'm here now and Mum's asked me to stay until you're better."

"I'm very tired," his father said.

"Of course you are. I'll go now and now let you sleep. I'll visit you with Mum tomorrow."

He thought about leaning over and giving his father a good night kiss, but he did not. His father closed his eyes and Joe watched him sleep for a while before he got up and slipped away.

He thanked the nurse at the desk, but he felt quite angry. The sheets in particular bothered him. The contrast between his father's bed and the bed he remembered from the two weeks he spent here was stark. His sheets had been bleached white and crisply starched with razor-sharp folds. He had loved watching the nurses make the bed each morning and then squeezing into the cool envelope, feeling the comforting tightness of the blankets. Everything in the ward was clean, scrubbed and disinfected. No woodlice crawling on his bed, no mice scratching against the skirting board, no rats scrabbling and squealing under the kitchen sink. He had loved the certainty of fixed mealtimes. Seven o'clock for a cup of tea and two slices of white bread. Breakfast at nine, cereal and a boiled egg with more white bread. Dinner at noon, perhaps a stew or meat and two veg, then tea at four. All the comics he could read. Crossword puzzles. Plenty of telly. And George Best.

Joe smiled at the memory. The doctor who had wheeled him down to the operating theatre had looked just like George Best with long black hair and beard. As Joe had felt himself slipping into a deep sleep, he had heard George telling him everything would be fine.

And when he had woken in the night, this throat and mouth parched with thirst, he had known that everything was fine. They had taken out his appendix. For a couple of days after the operation the wound had been very sore and he wasn't able to eat anything. And of course he had felt terrified that the doctors would find out the truth and expose him. He imagined George coming into the ward holding up a jar with the appendix suspended in liquid, his face darkening as he told Joe that what he had here was a healthy, perfectly normal fit-as-a-fiddle organ and that Joe was a little blackguard who had lied and wasted the doctors' and nurses' precious time. But as the days went by no such exposure took place and Joe began to relax, even to feel proud of his audacity.

The plan had germinated several years before when they were living in London and he had developed a pain in his side. His mother had taken him to the Whittington Hospital and the doctor had examined him, prodding his fingers gently into his abdomen and then slipping a gloved finger up Joe's anus to probe inside his rectum.

"Has he had a fever?" the doctor asked.

"No," Joe's mother had said.

"Any vomiting?"

"No".

The doctor had smiled: "There's nothing to worry about Mrs Hill. It's not an appendicitis, it's probably just indigestion."

"Thank you so much doctor," she had said. "Oh, and actually the name is Hill-Larkin, with a hyphen."

As they had left the hospital Joe had felt relief, but also some disappointment that he was not something for his mother to be worried about.

But Joe had filed the incident in his head. And this time he rehearsed his act fully. Step one was to complain of a pain in his side before going to his bed in the little room he shared with his brother. His mother had given him a teaspoon of Milk and Magnesia. Step two was to creep out early in the morning into the cold and damp kitchen and mix up a mug of cereal with some leftovers from the corned-beef hash they had eaten for their dinner with water and hurl this slop into the pan of the toilet. Step three was to splash cold water on his hair and face to give the appearance of sweat and tip toe back to bed where he lay with covers off, imagining a terrible pain radiating through his stomach.

Step four was to begin to groan and to turn and twist on the bed. He heard Daniel stir.

"What's the matter?", his little brother said sleepily from across the room.

"I'm not feeling good," Joe whimpered, and then let out a loud groan.

"Are you having a nightmare?" Daniel asked.

"No. I've got a pain. Owwwh," Joe went for broke with the groan.

"You're scaring me. Stop it."

"I'm going to be sick."

That did it.

"Mum!" Daniel shouted, tumbling out of bed and leaving the room. "Mum! Joseph's going to puke!"

Fooling his mother was easier than he had thought it would be. By the time she came into the room in her dressing gown, the pain in his side felt real and he did indeed feel feverish. As she examined him he began to shake. When his pyjama-clad father stumbled in, with the news that someone had vomited in the toilet, the deceit was complete and his mother took control. Ten minutes later they were in the Morris Oxford speeding down the dark, wet country lanes towards the town and the hospital.

The questions the doctor asked were the same as in London and the answers Joe gave and the cries of pain he emitted under the probing latex fingers made the diagnosis simple. "We will need to admit him, Mrs Hill-Larkin, for an operation. It's his appendix, so it is. It needs to be removed," the doctor said.

The Wards were still gathered around the entrance when Joe left. He put some distance between them then stopped to light a cigarette and look back at the buildings of the hospital. What a thing for an eleven year old to do, he thought sadly. What a terrible thing. There were so many questions stemming from his childhood which he wanted answered. His father was not in position to answer them. But maybe his mother was.

She was waiting for him when he reached the small pebble-dashed terraced house on the little side street behind the new shopping centre, and had opened the door before he had rang the bell. She reached up to embrace him. Joe stiffened but allowed her to put her arms round him. He patted her softly on the back. She felt very frail, like a bird, and he could feel her rib bones under her sweater. "How is your father?" she said.

"He's very tired and didn't have the energy to say very much so I let him sleep. But the nurses seem to be taking care of him," Joe replied.

"He's through the worst of it now. They say most people die in the first forty-eight hours. Do you want a cup of coffee?"

She led Joe into the large combined living room and kitchen which had been created by knocking through two smaller rooms. As she busied herself at the sink and cooker preparing the coffee, Joe looked around. The walls were covered with bookshelves which stretched to the ceiling. Books were crammed into shelves and piled on the floor alongside heaps of yellowing newspapers and cardboard boxes stacked with audio tapes. An old, battered and dusty orange sofa with a patchwork throw was positioned in the kitchen area next to an even more decrepit matching armchair which had moulded itself into the shape of his father.

A memory of the sofa and armchair, wrapped in shiny plastic, being delivered to their cottage in the country and the excitement he had felt crept into his head and then crept away again as he took in the rest of the furniture which consisted of a table with a grubby formica-top on which was set a jumble of overflowing ashtrays, unwashed cups

36

and a half cut loaf of soda bread, two wooden stools and a stack of discoloured white plastic garden chairs.

He walked over to the table. The floor was covered with a floral-print lino. It was swept but had not been washed for a long time and was sticky underfoot. He gathered up the cups and brought them to the draining board of the sink which was piled with dirty crockery. He emptied the ashtrays into an overflowing carrier bag of rubbish which sat on the floor and wiped crumbs and ash off the table with a slimy damp cloth. His mother waited until he created some order on the table and then handed him a mug of coffee. They both sat down at the table on the stools. His mother took a sip from her cup and lit a cigarette. Joe did the same.

"You're a good son Joseph. I'm so glad you came and so is your father," she said.

"Needs must," Joe said. "It was all a bit of shock to me. It must have been even worse for you."

"It was terrible", she said. Her head was nodding involuntarily and her eyes were watering. "I don't know what I would do if he died."

"He's not going to die Mum. He'll be right as rain in no time."

His mother smiled and blinked back her tears. "It was his hypochondria which saved him you know."

"How do you mean?"

"Well you know what your father's like. Always imagining the worst when he gets the slightest ache or pain and I don't have any sympathy for him. I need an aspirin he says and takes one while I tell him to stop being a big baby. The doctor says it was the aspirin he took before he collapsed which probably saved his life. It helped dissolve the clot in his heart. And there was me thinking all he had was indigestion."

"Good for Dad."

"Were the Wards at the hospital?"

"Yes. Just as you said they would be."

"It's a bad business. I wish I could do more to help."

"But how can you help?"

"The McDonagh's racket needs exposing. They're cowardly bullies. Once the other traveller families know what they're about and the corrupt politicians who support them are exposed, this gangsterism can be stopped. I've written a letter to the Connaught Tribune about it, but they haven't published it."

"I'd stay out of it if I was you Mum. It all sounds very dangerous."

"I can't remain stay silent on this issue. They want to shut me up, but they won't."

"Always the politico, eh? The tribune of the oppressed."

"If the world is going to be changed, the individual has to take action."

"I don't disagree. I just think you should let someone else take action. You've got enough on your plate."

"Oh Joseph, you're always so conservative. Don't you understand that by me doing something to help the Wards it helps me deal with what has happened to your father."

"But I still don't fully understand the connection."

"I've told you about the book I'm writing with Mary Ward."

"No. I thought you were working on a history of Jewish women in Ireland."

"I am, but I'm compiling an oral history of the travellers in the West as well. It's a collaboration with Mary. We've been collecting tape-recorded interviews for the last two years. We're going to call it "To Hell or To Connaught". That was Mary's idea, it's good don't you think."

"So you've got some recollections of Oliver Cromwell in there have you? Joe said, affecting a rough Irish brogue. "I was there when he rode his horse into St Nicholas's church and defiled the sacred altar. I was only a broth of a boy but my memory of the butchering blackguard remains as clear as the waters of the Corrib."

"Don't be faecetious, Joseph," she said smiling. "It's a serious work of history examining a rich cultural heritage which has been suppressed. The role of the family in traveller culture is fascinating."

"I'm sure it is," Joe said. He lit another cigarette. "Have you heard from Nathan?"

"I spoke to him while you were at the hospital. He's flying over tomorrow. I said if he wanted to stay for a while the two of you could make it into a little holiday. It's been so long since you've both been back."

"I'm not sure if I'm in a holiday mood," Joe said.

"It'll do me and your father good to know you're enjoying yourself. We don't want you behaving as if you're waiting for a wake. Now what would you like to do tonight?"

"What are you doing?"

"I need to visit Mary. Why don't you come. She'd be delighted to meet you."

"I'll pass on that if that's okay. I think maybe I need a little time on my own. I might go for a little walk."

"You do that. It'll be good for you. You'll be amazed at how our little town has changed in the last few years. The celtic Barcelona they're calling us. Who would have thought it."

"Are you sure you'll be safe visiting Mary?"

"Oh Joseph, she only lives round the corner and the McDonagh bully boys aren't interested in attacking women. It's the men they're after. But us women are going to put a stop to their little game."

Joe walked down Quay Street through a soft fine rain. The old stone warehouses he remembered lining the road had been turned into pizza restuarants and bars with fancy neon signs, poster promising the best craic in Ireland and bouncers on the doors. Crowds of boisterous young people spilled off the narrow pavement into the road.

Down at the quayside, by the spot-lit Spanish Arch, it was quieter and darker, and across the dock the lights of the Claddagh village glistened through the mizzle. The smell of the place had changed. The sea smelled fresh, not the stench of rotten seaweed which Joe remembered.

He walked onto the Wolf Tone Bridge over the Corrib and stopped to look over the parapet. The black roaring water was shot through with diamonds of silver from the reflections of the street lamps. In the spring time many years before he had stood here watching older boys snatch the salmon heading upstream with fishing lines and big treble-barbed hooks. The trick was to rip the hook deep into the belly of the fish so that it could be hauled up onto the bridge and finished off with a sharp blow.

The voice of his mother echoed in his head. Words she said two years before at the wake held for his grandmother, her mother. Elisha had been there.

"When I die Joseph, forget any notions of burial or cremation. I want to be sent floating down the Corrib dragging six bishops behind me. Can you arrange that for me?"

"Why would it be down to me to arrange?" Joe had replied. "It'd be up to Dad."

"Your father will die before me, that's why," she had said.

"It might be a bit difficult rounding up the bishops," Elisha had said with a smile, trying to lighten the conversation.

"Not at all. When they hear Rebecca Hill-Larkin, the scourge of Catholic hypocrisy, has kicked the bucket, they'll all come to the wake to gloat and you can just slip up behind them with a length of rope and tie them up. Get Nathan and Daniel to help. Then a little procession down to the river bank and in we all go. Now wouldn't that be grand?"

And Joe and Elisha had laughed; but afterwards they had wondered why.

The bright lights of the Roisin Dubh welcomed him. He entered the pub and slipped through a crowd of drinkers to the bar. Joe was approached immediately by a young barman in a white shirt and tie.

"Howya. What can I can do you for?" the barman asked.

Joe tried to scan the beer pumps.

"Have you got any draught premium lager?" he said.

"Heinekin."

"No I mean something over five per cent alcohol, like Becks or Grolsch."

"How about a bottle of Bud?"

"No. Just give us a pint of a Heinekin."

Joe took his pint and found a table in quiet corner. He took a sip of the lager and grimaced. It tasted like fizzy water. Across from him on the small stage a ceilidh band was preparing for a set. An accordion wheezed, a bodhran was thrumped and the strings of a fiddle scraped. Joe lit a cigarette and inhaled deeply. A torrent of thoughts surged through his head.

Accept them, Joe, he thought. Accept them as they are. I can't change the past. I can't change the way they are. But they're part of me. What does that say about me. I love them, but I hate them. I love myself, but I hate myself. Hardman Hill. Mr Control. JH for aggro. You mess with me and you get a boot in the bollocks.

"But you're a good son Joseph. You father is proud of you. We're both proud of you. We're especially proud of the lies. You're the best deceitful, dishonest, manipulating, conniving little blackguard we've had the fortune to bring into the world. Have a holiday. You and Nathan, the best of brothers, Cain and Abel." Me and Nathan. Dear old happy chappy Nathan. That kindly scowling face. Those gentle black knitted eyebrows. That charming, sneering, slurred skill at conversation. A magical, monosyllabic bundle of balding joy. Have a holiday. Let's go tripping over the hills of Connemara together. Me and Nathan. Two peas in pod. Blood is thicker than water. Am I my brother's keeper? I am my brother's keeper. The code, defend the code of honour, the code of the Hills, the debt of blood, honour thy father and thy mother. The Hills and the Wards united will never be defeated. Mad Dogs versus Englishmen. Mad Dog Nathan versus Joe Hard. "Fight! Fight! Fight!" You can take him Joe, you can take him."

Blood is thicker than water, but oil and water don't mix.

He saw the water of the Corrib, gently carrying the ribbon-festooned corpse of his mother, who was dragging behind her, by treble-barbed slash hooks knotted on ropes of tangled dirty sheets and plastic drip-tubes, his father, with his white hair spreading out across the river. Merrily, merrily, merrily, merrily, gently down the stream.

So the bullying of the McDonaghs had to be exposed? What about the history of the family you created mother dearest? Maybe someone needs to shine the searchlight of truth on that.

And then he heard a voice, a gentle, soft voice cutting through the clamour in his head. The voice of Elisha. "I love you Joe Hill. I love you for simply for being you and I love you for letting me be me."

Elisha. He had promised to ring her. She must be getting worried. Maybe he should have let her come with him. She had wanted to, but he couldn't do that to the one person in the world he loved, the one person who truly knew and loved him. This was his journey. Only he

41

could tread this road. But he had to ring her.

He went to the bar, ordered a double Jamesons and downed it one, then went to a telephone in an alcove. He dialled the number and poured change into the slot. The phone rang and rang. Just as he was about to replace the receiver, she answered.

"Hi, it's me," he said.

"How are you?" she said.

"I'm okay, Dad's okay," he said and felt a deep well of pain rising in his stomach.

"You don't sound okay," her voice was concerned, full of love.

"No," he said, his voice cracking. "I'm not okay. I'm not..."

A great bubble of hurt billowed up and exploded in a wracking sob. "It's so...It's so fucking terrible here. It's ...fucking...terrible. I just want...I want to ... I want to come home." And he let the great dam of tears inside him burst and engulf him.

A LIAR AND A THIEF

1
GROUNDWORK

J oe Hill took the spade off the hook on the wall of the shed and went to the raised bed at the back of his garden. The bed had been constructed with old railway sleepers, piled two-high, to form a 10-foot by 10-foot rectangle in which Joe had recently poured several hundredweight of bagged topsoil. The bed was Elisha's idea. She had demanded that something be done about the mess at this end of the garden. She had wanted structure. But now it was Joe's turn to get what he wanted.

He stepped up onto the bed and his boots sank slightly into the soil. The excavation he wanted was marked out with string. It had to be deep, at least waist high, deeper if possible. He sunk the spade into the ground and cleaved out the first spit and tossed it to one side. Within half an hour he had removed the topsoil. The going was harder now and he needed to apply his weight to cut through into the clay. It became easier to lift the heavy clods out with his hands and hurl them out than to lever them out with the spade.

It was a warm May day and he was sweating. He stopped to draw breath and to review progress. The mess Elisha so disliked was a mound of earth, shaded by sycamore trees, on which nothing but weeds flourished. Joe had tried planting a variety of shade-loving plants but the structure to satisfy Elisha had never materialised. Underneath the mound was rubble, possibly from an Anderson shelter or possibly from the remains of a shed. The road they lived on was shed city. Most of their neighbours had at least two sheds. Next door had six of varying ages and constructions. Joe and Elisha had one shed, which was slowly rotting because Joe had not yet got round to fixing its leaking roof.

Joe thought about the next stage of digging. What worried him most was finding animal life down in the rubble. A family of mangy city foxes frequented the area and Joe had spotted them sunning themselves on his lawn. Foxes lived in burrows and the ruins of an air raid shelter would have made a perfect habitat.

Rats also liked living underground. And he had seen one in the garden as well. It had come skulking along the line of the fence while Joe was hoeing a border on the other side of the garden. Joe had frozen in terror. The rat didn't notice him and continued its path towards the shed. Then, to Joe's relief, his neighbour's fat tabby cat appeared behind the rat, stalking it. The rat must have smelled the cat for it turned round and reared up on its hind legs, its claws ready to strike. To Joe's horror the cat fled. The rat gave chase. Joe broke out of his paralysis and looked for weapons. The hoe was too puny for close quarter combat with a rat. In fact, Joe did not want to be close to the rat at all. He spotted some pebbles and gathered them instead and went after the combatants. The cat had jumped up on the fence and the victorious rat was heading back towards Joe. Joe lobbed a pebble. It bounced over the rat. He skimmed another. Again he missed. Perhaps, emboldened by Joe's actions, the cat decided to re-enter the fray and pounced. He missed his target. The rat scurried under the fence. The cat leapt over the fence in pursuit. Joe was relieved, but soon he got to thinking about why the rat was heading for the shed in the first place. Had it created a home there? For its family?

He thought about the risk of uncovering a rat's family home as he began levering out old bricks and chunks of concrete from the clay. His fear of rats stemmed from childhood. Mother said it began when Joe volunteered to look after the school hamster during the Easter holidays and had kept the cage in his bedroom. Both parents had to come in to comfort him when they had found him screaming in the middle of night, saying that the hamster was coming to eat him. But of more significance to Joe was the island in a lake in the West of Ireland, which his parents had bought as a holiday home when Joe was five and they were flush with cash from the success of a play they had written. They had built a wooden flat-roofed house on concrete stilts in the middle of eight acres of scrub, woods and limestone rock which lay a quarter of a mile from the mainland.

When they left at the end of their first summer the rats moved in. They swam the distance from the mainland, climbed up the concrete posts and gnawed through the floor. On the family's return the following year they opened the door of the house to find a scene of devastation. The rats had burrowed into the mattresses on the beds, soaked them with piss and strewn the horsehair innards across the floor. They had chewed their way into the food cupboards and raided the bags of flour, rice and sugar. They had scaled the bookcases and made confetti out of the paperbacks. Their rampage through the house was marked by trails of centimetre-long grains of black shit. And the scent of rat was everywhere. A pungent mustiness cut through with the acridity of urine. Joe's family had spent a day cleaning up the mess. Father then attempted to make the place rat proof. Tin sheet was nailed over the corners of the floor where the rats had gnawed through. Metal dustbins were bought to store the food. And poison was laid under the house. A few rats took the bait and Joe would come across their bodies in the woods, stiff with rigour mortis, congealed blood around their open jaws. But the remainder just waited. And at night, as Joe lay in his bunk bed throughout the summer, he thought he could hear them scurrying about under the floor, climbing up the concrete posts and scratching at the metal sheets trying to find a way in.

The hole was now waist deep and the last traces of rubble had been removed. Joe went round stomping with his boots to firm the base of the excavation and the shelves he had cut into the walls. He sat down and admired his work. The smell of the damp earth was comforting. He heard a footfall above him and then Elisha's smiling face poked over the rim of the hole.

"Having fun?" she said.

"Yes, thank you," Joe replied.

"Are you sure it's deep enough?"

"Deep enough to bury you in."

"That's not a nice thing to say."

"This is my hole and I don't need you criticising it."

"I wasn't criticising. I was just asking a question. I was going to ask you if you wanted a cup of tea, but I don't think I'll bother now. And when you do come in, try not to get mud all over the carpet. You're covered in it."

Elisha's face disappeared. Joe thought about standing up in his hole and calling after her to apologise, but he decided against it.

"Try not to get mud on the carpet." That is what Mother said when he had been out in the garden making complicated lines of trenches and shell holes for his plastic First World War soldiers. Instead of praising his intricate recreation of the Western Front, which included barbed wire entanglements made from fuse wire, sandbags fashioned from used tea bags and duck boards made with lollipop sticks, she had belittled his efforts. "You're making such a mess of my flower bed Joseph. I do hope you clear it up before you come in." And then as she left, as if taking a cue, Joe's older brother, Nathan, appeared. "Incoming Howitzer barrage!" he screamed and started jumping on and kicking the trenches until Joe's toy soldiers were obliterated by mud. And once the destruction of the earthworks was complete, Nathan began kicking Joe in the shins and slapping him round the head while chanting: "You've made such a mess Joseph." And when Joe tried to fight back, Nathan threw him to the ground and buried his face in the mud, until Joe thought he was going to suffocate. When he eventually staggered indoors with the tears streaming down his blackened face all Mother had to say was "Oh Joseph, look at the state of you. Get to the bathroom this instant."

Back in the house, after taking off his mud-caked boots and cleaning his hands, Joe came up behind Elisha and put his arms around her waist.

"I'm sorry I was grouchy with you. But digging the hole bought back some childhood memories," he said, kissing her on the back of the neck.

"Do you want to talk about it?"

"I dunno what there is to talk about," Joe said, sitting down at the kitchen table.

Elisha sat opposite him. "Well, what sort of childhood memories?"

"Oh I dunno. Stuff with my brother. Living on the island. My phobias. The mess I've made of my life. That sort of thing."

"Go on."

"Oh Christ, I don't know, Elisha. It's just that everything I do seems to turn out wrong. I'm in the wrong job. I've forced you to live in an area you hate. We seem to spend more time arguing and fighting than having any pleasure." He saw her eyes harden.

"I don't want to hear this Joe. Yes I hate living in Walthamstow. It's a shithole. But I made a choice in coming here. In the same way you made a choice about your job. We fight because you're not open to me about how you're feeling. You close off to me. And I can't stand that."

"But how can that be. I'm trying to be open with you now, but you're saying you don't want to hear it. I can't win."

"But you're not saying what you're feeling. You're just coming out with the usual generalisations. You've got to do some work here, if you want me to listen."

"Right, I'll do some work. Digging the hole made me think of how awful my childhood was. How every summer I had to endure a terror about rats. About how my mother used to disparage everything I did. How I could do nothing right. How my brother used to inflict violence and torture on me and my parents did nothing. Shall I go on?"

"No. I've told you before Joe. You need to say all this to a therapist. That's what I'm doing. And it's very hard and very painful. But it's the only way of moving forward."

"I'm not going to see a bloody therapist." Joe said, getting up from the table.

"Where are you going?"

"Back to my hole."

"Well go to back to your bloody hole!"

Joe went back out into the garden and stood over his hole. He felt the anger churning up inside him. There was no point talking to Elisha. She played mind games with him. Whatever he said was wrong. Of one thing he was certain. No way would he see a therapist. He had seen what therapy had done to Elisha. It had almost destroyed her and him too in the process. No, what he needed was a sense of himself, as a man, as a creator. And this project he had set himself was a means to that end. He would build a pond, a beautiful pond. It was something he truly wanted.

Elisha's acceptance of his idea of creating a pond had come as a pleasant surprise. They were visiting a garden show at Alexandra Palace. It had cost £30 for both of them to enter the event and the publicity for it had led them to expect a mini-version of the Chelsea Flower show. They were sadly disappointed. Most of the space in the Great Hall and adjoining rooms were taken up by companies selling garden accessories, expensive lighting systems, even more expensive jacuzzis, tropical hardwood furniture and landscape design services. The handful of show gardens created were tiny and uninspiring under the artificial light of the venue. There was also little to stimulate in the collection of flowers and shrubs on display. After shuffling around the exhibition, they went for a drink in the adjoining Phoenix Bar.

"Well that was a rip off," Joe said. "Could just as well have sent off for a catalogue."

"I liked the cannas. I thought they might go at the back." Elisha said.

"There's not enough light."

"But we've got to do something. It's a mess. It's horrible. It needs some structure."

"What about a pond?"

"A pond?"

"I think a pond would go brilliantly there. It would provide a focal point. We could plant interesting shade-loving plants around it. Hostas, ferns, succulents, maybe even some bamboo."

"What made you think of a pond?"

"I dunno. It's just come to me. But I want one. We could put fish in it and have a fountain."

"But I can't see how it would work."

"Look, I'll show you. Have got a pen and some paper?"

Now as Joe stood looking at his hole and the mounds of excavated earth and rubble surrounding it, he felt a pang of self-doubt as to whether the actuality of his project would match that vision. As darkness fell, he returned to the house, knowing that for the moment at least, some form of reparation with Elisha took priority.

2
ANGER

A t work, Joe opened a spreadsheet. Columns of figures streamed down the page, the results of a student satisfaction survey. Except you couldn't use the word student now, thought Joe. Now that they were paying fees and racking up thousands of pounds in debt, students had become customers. It was double speak. As soon as the word customer started to be deployed you could guarantee that the person so designated would be treated like shit. It was like the tube. In the past when the trains ran frequently without delay and when the signals and escalators worked, Joe was called a passenger. Now as he endured the daily sweaty crush and uncertainty of travelling into work, he had become a customer.

He reviewed the findings of survey. 60 per cent of students were satisfied with the physical condition of their learning environment. 20 per cent were dissatisfied. 20 per cent didn't know. Didn't know, he thought. How could they not know? And how could 60 per cent be satisfied? The university buildings were a hell hole. A mixture of mouldering Victorian Gothic and crumbling 1960's concrete. The old buildings were freezing in winter and stifling hot in summer; the modern ones were suffocatingly hot all year round.

He opened the window in front of his desk. On the road below, in a blue haze of exhaust fumes, traffic inched its way past yet another excavation for cabling towards the City. A workman in the cab of a JCB revved his engine to begin another morning of jack hammering. Joe shut the window. The university was ugly, but the world outside was even uglier.

He minimised the spreadsheet and tapped creating ponds into the Google search box. He clicked on the first name in the list – wet&wild. com – and an animated image of a woman urinating loaded. He hit the back button fast. The next site on the list looked more promising

– pondworld.co.uk – all you need to know to build a perfect pond. He entered the site. An hour later, Joe checked the weather forecast. It was not good. The next two days would be fine, but rain and wind was on the way and the weekend looked like being a washout. He picked up the phone and rang the extension of Judith, his manager. Pat, her PA answered.

"Is she there?" Joe asked.

"No Joe, she's working at home," Pat said. "Alright for some isn't it. Can I help?"

"I'm not feeling too good. I think I'm coming down with the vomiting virus."

"Oh poor you. My daughter had that last week. It's not nice. It started with the squits and then she starting chucking up. She made a right mess of my carpet."

"Pat, do you need to go into the details?"

"Sorry. But don't worry, she was right as rain within three days. You need to drink plenty of water."

"Thanks for the advice. Could you mark me down as sick?"

"Course I will darling. Now you go home and rest up."

Leaving work, Joe felt a sense of liberation. It was easy. No one would question him. He smiled as a memory came into his head. An early morning when he didn't want to go to school. Creeping into the kitchen and mixing up a mess of cereal and the leftovers of last night's dinner with water in a cup and then chucking it into the toilet pan. Scooping up the dregs with his fingers and smearing the mix on his chin and then rubbing a bit of cold water through his hair leaving droplets on his forehead before staggering into his parents' bedroom to say: "Mother, I'm not feeling well." And she bought it. The vomit in the toilet was the deciding factor, earning him a day of peace in bed reading comics and eating grapes.

On the way back on the tube Joe planned his next steps. He came out of Walthamstow Central in brilliant sunshine and his spirits soared as he walked through the cats-cradle of streets north of market admiring the daffodils, tulips and pansies blooming in the little front gardens of the red-brick terraced houses.

Reaching his own house, he opened the front door and went through to the kitchen. The door to the garden was open. Joe's first thought was burglars, but as he stepped outside he saw Elisha down at the end of the garden with a man who was inspecting the hole he had dug. Joe recognised him as Roger Barton, an English teacher who used to work at Elisha's school. As he walked down to join them, Elisha gave him a puzzled look and Roger grinned.

"What are you doing here?" Elisha said.

"I decided to go sick? What are you doing here, I thought you were on an Inset?"

"We were, but the trainer cancelled at the last minute and Roger gave me a lift back. What's the matter with you?"

"Nothing. Just fancied some time off. Hello Roger."

"Hello Joe," Roger said and stuck out his hand for Joe to shake. "Nice seeing you again."

"I thought you'd quit teaching and were travelling round the world on your motor bike?" Joe said.

"I did, but the bloody thing packed in while I was doing the Inca Way in Peru and so I came back. I decided I missed the masochistic pleasure of being abused by stroppy teenagers. Plus I needed the cash."

"Well, I think you're bonkers," Elisha said to Roger.

"Not as bonkers as the people in my new department. Do you remember Henry?"

"Oh God, do I? He tried to strangle the deputy head."

"Well he's my head of department," he said chuckling. "It's a madhouse."

Joe looked at the laughter in Elisha's eyes and did not like it. "Do you want some tea?" he asked Roger.

"That would be fantastic," Roger said.

"What about you, darling?" Joe said to Elisha.

"Yeah okay," she said, but without much warmth.

Joe walked back to the kitchen. He had met Roger on a few occasions, mainly in the pub down the road from Elisha's school. He had a passion about life and a reputation as an inspirational teacher. Elisha had told him how Roger had once taken a class of the saddest, baddest and maddest 14-year-olds in the school, many of them refugees from African and Middle East war zones where they had experienced terrible things, which was acted out in the class room in violence against each other and against the teachers. And to these terribly damaged kids, Roger had introduced Paradise Lost and told them the story of how Milton had written the poem while he was going blind and how his eyesight had steadily disappeared until all he could see was a little chink of light, but how this did not stop him completing the epic poem. And the kids were captivated by this and they had told all their other teachers about John Milton and his chink of light.

Roger also had a reputation as a ladies man. According to Elisha, he had charmed the knickers off a considerable proportion of women staff at the school, from class room assistants to senior teachers. They went for his combination of strong earthy masculinity (he had once told Elisha that he never washed with soap) and his emotional honesty. This emotional honesty usually entailed telling his latest conquest that he was ending the relationship for their sake, to stop them getting hurt. He had also admitted to Elisha that he didn't like wearing underpants as they constrained him and that he preferred going commando.

Joe came out with three mugs balanced on a tin tray to find Roger with his nose buried in the candyfloss bloom of a lilac tree. He inhaled deeply and turned to Joe.

"Fantastic. I love lilac. Reminds me of Proust. La Recherche du Temps Perdu."

"That's what I thought when I planted it," said Elisha.

"Have you read Proust?" Roger asked Joe.

"I tried to. A bit florrid for me. Too many words," Joe replied handing out the mugs.

"Oh no," Roger said. "It's like poetry. Everyone word counts in all of the 20 volumes. Absolutely fantastic." He took a sip of sip tea. "Eli says you're building a pond? Mind if I take a look?"

"You should ask Roger's advice Joe. He knows a lot about ponds. He'll tell you if you're doing it right," Elisha said.

Joe stifled his rising anger and said. "I'd welcome any advice."

Roger walked over to the hole, kicked at the edges and then jumped down inside it. "You're doing well. But I would make it a bit deeper if I was you. You're having fish right?"

Joe nodded.

"Well if it's only this depth the water will freeze solid in winter and you'll have fish fingers. You need to dig out about another two feet. You'll also run into problems unless you get the edges level. Chuck me a spade and I'll show you how."

"Nah, that's alright. Why don't you continue your nice chat with Elisha. I was planning to go to Homebase to get a lining."

"There's a bit of an art to putting the lining in. You need to get the folding right."

"I think I'll manage," said Joe walking away and giving Elisha a dirty look.

3
PROJECTION

"Fuckwit," Joe thought, as he wheeled his trolley through the aisles of Homebase. You're a bullshitter, Roger. There aren't 20 volumes of In Search of Lost Time, there's only seven. And you're a bullshitter too Elisha. You didn't plant the lilac. I did. You just sat in a fucking director's chair supervising me. "

The anger was boiling up in him and he felt tempted to ram the metal trolley into the fat backside of the woman who was dithering in front of the paint shelves, blocking his way. Instead he manoeuvred the trolley sharply around her, clipping her leg in the process. The woman yelped.

"Terribly sorry," said Joe, driving on and smiling. But then he heard a howling behind him and turned to see the woman had crumpled to the floor and was holding her calf. Blood was spilling out through her fingers and onto the floor. He stopped the trolley and started walking back but several other customers got to her first.

"It's my varicose vein," the woman whimpered. "That man cut my varicose vein."

The other customers turned to look at Joe.

"It was an accident," he pleaded. "It's the bloody trolleys in this place. They're wheels are wonky. Here let me help. I know first aid."

"Stay away from me!" the woman screamed.

A shop assistant carrying a first aid box pushed through the gathering crowd around the woman. Joe backed away.

"Trolley rage," he heard a woman say. "Men like that get sight of a power tool and get all aggressive."

Joe hurried away to the garden section where it took him half an hour to find everything he needed. By the end of the expedition his trolley was fully laden and he was £500 out of pocket.

Elisha was sitting at the kitchen table marking a large pile of workbooks when he staggered through carrying a large bag of sand. She looked at him coldly but did not speak. After he had made a fifth trip through to the garden and dumped his last purchase, the solar powered fountain, he came back into the kitchen and stood in front of her, panting.

"Roger gone?" he asked.

"What's it to you?"

"No need to snap at me."

"You were very rude."

"I thought I was very polite, considering…"

"Considering what?"

"Considering he's a patronising bastard and he's full of bullshit. 'Oh Eli this is fantastic. Reminds me of Proust'. Bollocks. I don't believe he's read In Search of Lost Time. I know for a fact that there aren't 20 volumes. There are only seven."

"Oh stop being pathetic. You're just jealous."

"Jealous? Jealous of what? Jealous of a man who doesn't wear underpants?"

"What is it with you and underpants? Why does it bother you if someone doesn't wear them?"

"Because it's unhygienic, that's why."

"You're repressed Joe. You're repressed and you're jealous of someone who's passionate about life and you're not. You know something? I'm sick of you and your depression and insecurities. You're like a bloody great damp black cloud every time you come into the house, spreading misery everywhere."

"I'm very passionate about life. What makes me miserable is you. What's this?" Joe said, picking up a brown and grey striped woolly rug which was draped on a chair.

"It's a present from Roger."

"But what is it?"

"It's a llama throw. Now put it down before you dirty it."

"So who's worried about hygiene now?" He sniffed the throw. "Have you smelt it? It smells like rotten cheese. Roger's probably been using it to wipe his foreskin."

"Oh stop being so bloody childish."

Joe put the rug down. "Look. I didn't take the day off today to have a fight with you. I've got things to do," he said, walking out into the garden.

Once back in the hole, Joe attacked the bottom with a spade. He recognised that Roger was right about the depth but, with every inch of clay he hacked out, hated him for being right.

Elisha's hypocrisy was outstanding. She was the one who told him about Roger's lack of underpants and personal hygiene and now she had turned it round so that he was the one who was repressed. Of course he didn't have a problem with underpants. It was the lack of them that bothered him.

Mother had never appreciated the importance of underpants and was quite content to let him go to infants school without them. This hadn't concerned Joe until the nativity play when he had been picked to play one of the wise men. Joe had run home all excited and had told Mother that she would need to make his costume. She fashioned a tunic out of an orange-and-brown-striped cushion cover from the battered sofa in the living room and made him an Arab headdress out of a tea towel and a length of curtain cord. Joe tried the costume on and was told that he looked the part and he had bought it into school in a bag and given it to his teacher for safe keeping until the afternoon of the performance. Rehearsals were conducted in normal school clothes, which in Joe's case was a pair of blue ski pants and a jumper.

When the big day came, a classroom was turned into a dressing room and the teachers helped each child get ready. Joe slipped into his tunic and began putting on his headdress when a teacher came across and said: "You will need to take your trousers off, Joe. The wise men didn't wear ski pants." "Can't I keep them on?" Joe had asked, hearing giggles from the girl playing Mary who was standing next to him. "No, you will look silly, Joe. Now you don't want to look silly in front of your Mum and Dad, do you?" It was with mortification that Joe complied and carefully pulled his trousers down making sure that no one could see that he wasn't wearing underpants. "That's better" said the teacher. But it didn't feel that way to Joe. He felt extremely vulnerable, a vulnerability which turned to shame once he climbed the stage in the assembly and found himself looking down on the audience; an audience who were all in a prime position to look up his tunic. He could still feel the shame now, despite the passage of time. His little private parts had been put on display to be laughed at and his mother had allowed it happen. Instead of the opportunity to show his acting potential, the little Joe was reduced to trembling at the back of the stage with his knees tightly pressed together.

He banished the memories and focused on straightening the edges of the pond, using a spirit level to get them right. He then unrolled the black PVC pond liner and laid it out on the lawn. The liner was thinner than he had expected and he questioned whether the sand he had bought would be sufficient to use as a protective base to stop stones coming through the soil and puncturing it.

Elisha came out. "I'm going to the shops. Do you want anything?"

"No."

He watched her go back up the garden and thought hard until his lips formed a mischievous smile. After a few minutes, when he was sure she was out of the house, he went into the kitchen. He grabbed the Peruvian llama rug from the chair and bought it outside. He opened a bag of sand, shovelled it into the base of the hole and then smoothed it out with his feet. He placed the rug on top of the sand and patted it into the contours of the hole. It fitted perfectly. He lowered the liner on top of the rug and carefully pushed it so that it fitted the hole snugly. He then unrolled and turned on his garden hose and began filling the hole with water. As the weight of the water pulled the PVC tight, he made careful folds in the liner around the sides.

By the end of the day Joe was exhausted but happy. The basics of the pond were there. He sat until darkness drinking beer and admiring his craftsmanship.

4
DENIAL

Elisha was marking at the kitchen table when Joe came indoors. He ignored her, went through to the living room and slumped on the sofa in front of the TV. He felt very tired and closed his eyes.

He awoke to find his hair being wrenched from his scalp. Elisha stood over him.

"Where is it? Tell me where it is?"

Joe tried to grab her wrists but she twisted his head around. He felt the skin on his face being stretched. "Let go for Christ's sake."

"Not until you've told me what you've done with it."

"I don't know what you're talking about. Please let go of me."

She relaxed her pull for second and Joe twisted free, feeling some of his hair being ripped out in process. He rolled over onto the floor and scrambled up as Elisha advanced on him. He pushed his palms out to ward her off.

"Elisha stop. Just stop."

"Roger's present. What have you done with it?" Her fists were balled and her eyes were blazing.

"I haven't done anything with it. Where did you leave it?"

"It was on the kitchen chair and now it's gone. You've done something with it. I know you have."

"I swear to God I haven't."

"There are only two of us in this house. I didn't move it. So you must have done."

"I didn't. Maybe a fox came in and took it."

"A fox? Why would a fox take a llama throw?"

"It might have thought it was a dead animal. You know how badly it smelt." Joe tried to stifle a smile.

"Don't laugh at me Joe. This isn't funny."

Joe advanced with his arms open. "Elisha, look. I promise you, I didn't touch the throw. I swear. It's probably around somewhere. Let me help you look for it."

"Why is it I don't believe you?"

"I don't know. Look this is silly." He tried to embrace her.

"Don't touch me." There were tears welling up her eyes. "I want that throw back. Do you hear." She broke away from him and left the room slamming the door.

Joe sat on the sofa and rubbed head. His scalp was very tender. The ferocity of the attack shocked him. And also the fact that she had caught him unawares. It was like the time his parents had confronted him about stealing money. He was nine years old.

The trigger for his crime wave had been a bus journey he had taken with Mother. On the wooden floor of the red Routemaster, he had spotted a crumpled blue five pound note. He had put his foot on it and dragged it near before snatching it up. Excitement flooded through him. He was rich. He had nudged Mother and unballed his fist to let her see his find. She had smiled.

"Oh Joseph, aren't you lucky."

"Finder's keepers, loser's weepers?"

"Finder's keepers. But it's a lot of money, Jospeh, why don't you let me look after it. I'll keep it safe for you in my purse."

"But I'll be able to buy stuff won't I?"

"Of course you will darling. We'll go to the toy shop together."

Joe had handed over the note and began to imagine what he could buy. He decided on a whole model army, but not plastic, metal. Lifeguards with shiny helmets and breastplates on white horses, Grenadier Guardsmen standing tall in their bearskins led by a drummer in a leopard-skin, kilted Black Watch Highlanders with bagpipers, Indian troops in turbans and, best of all, cannon drawn by teams of four horses, perfectly detailed down to the miniature ram rods, cartridges and water buckets attached on little hooks on the underside of the gun carriages. That night, he could hardly sleep with excitement.

But the next day all Mother had allowed him to buy was one cannon with a gun carriage and two horses. After the man in the shop wrapped the cannon, they went home, with Mother saying how lucky he was; Joe, silent and seething.

His revenge was subtle and protracted. Every day when he had the opportunity he went to Mother's purse and stole some pennies. He calculated that she probably counted the notes and the silver but not the coppers. He began hoarding the pennies in a jam jar, which he hid under a broken floorboard beneath his bed. As the jar filled, he gained in confidence. Soon he was taking money from the purses of Mother's friends when they visited and then from the mothers of his own friends. He graduated from coppers to silver and then to £1 notes. Soon he needed a bigger jar. At night under the cover of darkness using a small pocket torch he unearthed his cache and allowed the light to play over the shiny treasure within.

He spent his treasure carefully at first, on sweets to hand out at school. But then he got bold. His best friend Raymond came into school with a brand new Timex with a leather strap. Megan Rowlands, who both Raymond and Joe fancied, was very impressed. Joe wanted her to be impressed with him and on a Saturday he retrieved the handful of pound notes from his stash and went to the jewellers on the high street. The next Monday in school he proudly showed Megan and Raymond his new Timex, which had an expandable steel bracelet like James Bond's watch. Megan transferred her affections to him. He was careful for the next few days and made sure that he took the watch off before coming into the house and then hid it in his cache. But on the Friday he forgot and Mother saw it.

"Where did you get the watch, Joseph?"

"Oh my pal Raymond's just bought a new watch and he let me have his old one."

"It looks very new to me."

"That's because he got it as a Christmas present. But he got a better one as a birthday present and so he gave it to me."

The matter was left at that and Joe though his explanation had been good. That night as he lay in bed, he heard raised voices from downstairs. He could only make out snippets.

"You've got to do something Jeffery."

"Now don't get me upset, Rebecca."

"This can't go on. You've got to act."

The voices stopped and Joe curled up to go to sleep. Then the door to his bedroom crashed open.

"Where's the money Joseph?" Mother screamed.

"Tell your mother, Joseph," Father said.

Mother came over the bed, she was spitting with anger. "You thieving little brat, I know you've got it hidden here."

She grabbed the mattress and turfed Joe out of bed. As he cowered on the floor Father knelt down and grabbed his pajama jacket. "We know you weren't given that watch Joseph. Now tell your mother where the money is?"

Mother had upended the bed and was scrabbling on the floor. She ripped up the loose floorboard and put her hand into the hole.

"I've found it Jeffrey. I've found it!"

Over the course of the weekend, Joe tried to explain about the injustice of the five pound note. His parents had none of it. He was a liar and a thief and that was all there was to it. For punishment they stopped his pocket money for two years.

A liar and a thief. Joe rubbed his head. No longer a thief but still a liar. Using the llama throw to line the pond was childish but it was done now. There was no way that he could be expected to empty the pond and remove the liner. But if he told Elisha that is exactly what she would expect him to do. Maybe he would tell her when things had cooled down. They could have a laugh about it. It was only a smelly rug after all.

5
CLOSURE

It was May again. It had been a miserable wet winter but now it seemed as if summer had arrived. Joe sat in a director's chair basking in the warm sunshine, sipping a can of ice-cold Grolsch and gazing meditatively at the pond. The solar-powered fountain was sending up a three-foot spray of water crystals in which a mini rainbow shimmered. The downward drops of water splashed on the lush leaves of an iris, rocking its delicate purple flowers and puckered the surface of the pond. In the clear water a little gold orfe nosed gently, feeding on insect larvae. In the corner of the pond, protected by the overhanging paving stones, two frogs poked their heads above the water and kept watch on the black tadpoles darting around the edges. Ribbed leaves of hostas bowed down towards the water. Small insects, pond skaters and water-boat-men flitted across the surface. Above in the trees, Joe heard the song of blackbirds.

Joe drained his lager and crushed the can in his fist. He had created a pond and it was a beautiful pond, but it was all meaningless. The whole point to creating beauty was to share it, but his action with the llama throw, the foundation of his pond, had lost him the one person with whom he wanted to share his creativity.

The smelly rug had achieved a kind of monumental symbolism. Its disappearance turned the cracks of distrust and anger between him and Elisha into a chasm. He couldn't admit his lie and Elisha couldn't tolerate his dishonesty. His attempts after the attack to make things better had been treated with even more distrust until he began to feel that his feelings for Elisha were also one big lie.

They lived together in the house for a while in angry silences. Joe spent more and more time in the garden consolidating the pond and Elisha spent more and more time in the pub after work. In late July she went on holiday on her own. In August she moved out and Joe was left with his pond.

GHOST STORIES

THE OULD ONE

I lived in Ireland as a teenager in a little village called Corrandulla. In the 1970s our cottage, like many others, did not have running water or electricity. O'Shea's – an old thatched pub set back from the Tuam Road and overlooking a racing stream which fed into Lough Corrib – did and I was in there for a lock-in one cold December night. In those days many Irish landlords had no qualms about serving 15-year-olds like myself. As I sat in warm fug of the bar, supping a pint of Harp lager, listening to a fiddler and a bodhran player, I noticed the landlord take a bowl of buttermilk and a little plate with a large slice of barm brack and place them on the hearth of the turf fire.

As he passed me on the way back to the bar, I asked him: "Why are you doing that Seamus?"

"It's to keep the Ould One out of my bed," he replied.

"The Ould One?" I said, thinking maybe it was his cat or his dog. "What sort of beast is that?"

"It's no beast," he said. "It's the ghost of an ould woman. Unless I leave the buttermilk and barm brack by the fire, she'll be crawling in my bed tonight and Jaysus her hands are terribly cold."

"You're codding me," I said.

"Oh no," he said. "I swear by the Sacred Heart it's true. And it's been my misfortune to forget on a few occasions."

"But why would she want to get in your bed?" I asked.

"She's cold with hunger. Back in 1847, during the blackest time in the Great Famine, the poor starving wretches of the parish came down to the stream to eat the watercress which grows by the banks. And when that was gone, they ate the grass. By December there were corpses left out there in the cold with the green juice of the grass frozen on their lips, and the Ould One was one of them. Except her body was found right outside this bar. She'd been scratching her finger nails on the door begging to be let in, but my great grandda, may the Lord have mercy on him, refused to unbolt the door."

"And how does she get in?" I said.

"Whist, for the life of me I don't know," he said. "I would lock all the doors and windows before I went to bed, including the door to my bedroom, but still she would creep in. And it wasn't just the icy cold of her bony body that put the bejasus up me, it was the smell. She reeks of rotting vegetation."

"Christ! Does she say anything when she hops into bed with you?"

"Not a word. She comes under the covers all silent, but for someone that emaciated she doesn't half have a grip in those scrawny arms, it's like she's trying to squeeze the life out of me."

I left O'Shea's and walked along the road by the stream. There was a full moon and I could see the swirls of watercress in the water. But then, as I approached the ruins of the old mill, I saw a shape coming slowly towards me. It was crawling on all fours. I froze. Hot piss trickled down my leg. I wanted to run but my legs had turned to jelly. The moonlight caught the white of bony face and a set of crooked teeth. I instinctively began to recite what I could remember from my only visit to church.

"Hail Mary, full of Grace, the Lord is with you
Blessed art thou amongst women
And blessed is the fruit of thy womb, Jesus."

A terrible acrid stench filled the air. Two mournful big eyes shone through the dark and advanced on me. I heard a pitiful long-drawn out groan and clasped my hands together.

"Holy Mary, mother of God, pray for us sinners
Now and at the hour of our death..."

Then finally the creature reached me. I saw four spindly legs and a matted grey-white fleece and breathed a sigh of relief. It was a sheep. A fecking sheep!

SHADOW OF THE SCARECROW

It was the night before Epiphany and the snow was smothering the allotments of Craggy Farm. An icy wind from Siberia had driven the rats and foxes into their burrows and no sensible human dared venture out. Only one dark figure appeared to brave the elements.

On plot 39, a scarecrow's face was thrust defiantly into the blizzard. But apart from the wind-blown fluttering of his black rags, he showed no sign of movement and his eyes appeared dead. A large crow hopped from the cover of the bramble bush behind the scarecrow and began pecking through the snow in the search for grubs. The scarecrow's nostrils twitched and then suddenly flared.

Jacob Mortly surveyed his plot. Yesterday's wind had dropped, the snow flurries had stopped and a thaw was setting in. He crunched along the path between his raised beds to inspect his brussel sprouts. Although the outer leaves were blackened by the cold, the hearts were not frozen. Excellent, he thought, a touch of frost worked wonders with the flavours of a sprout. But something was wrong. He looked at his scarecrow. "What bugger's moved you Black Jake?" he said.

He pondered the fact that the scarecrow's position had changed from in front of the bramble hedge running along the right hand path of the plot to the left hand side in front of his onion bed. Was it yobs from outside or someone from inside the allotment? Either way he suddenly felt threatened. Teenage yobs who didn't know better he could understand. A good clip round the ear or a three-pronged fork up the backside would sort them out. But someone from the allotment? That was different. He needed to investigate.

He walked carefully towards the scarecrow scanning the snow for footprints. But apart from the imprint of some birds feet, there was nothing. He turned to where he had positioned the scarecrow. No footprints, but there was something else. He shuddered. The snow was red with blood. Not just blood but blue black feathers scattered in a circle. And worse, the glistening entrails of a crow and it's severed head with a beady dead eye staring at him. Fox! he thought. But where were the paw prints? And why hadn't the fox eaten the entrails as they usually did? It was all very strange.

Jacob Mortly moved closer to his scarecrow to see if any damage had been done. Nothing. He was still in as good a condition as when he had freecycled him from Catweazle's plot the previous January.

Catweazle, who was universally disliked on the allotment, had keeled over with a heart attack on plot 69 and was stiff with rigour mortis by the time the allotment secretary Barbara Pymm had found him wedged between his curly kale. As was the tradition on the allotment, the other plot holders had divvied up his goods following the funeral and after it become clear that Catweazle had no family or at least no family who were interested in him. Barbara Pymm didn't like this tradition and said the men were like vultures scavenging the remains of the dead, but Jacob thought it was a fine tradition which fitted well with this going-green-thing the youngsters spouted off about. His thoughts were interrupted by a snarl behind him. He span round, fists clenched. Adrenalin kicking in for a fight or flight defence. It was a fox. An angry, hungry mangy fox.

The fox's sharp teeth were bared and smeared with blood. A glistening strand of crow intestine dangled from the side its mouth. Jacob kept his position but shifted his weight to take up a more stable fighting stance. If the fox came out at him low, he would kick; if came high, he would punch. He tried to relax his breathing but a familiar voice distracted his focus.

"You're not scared of Old Renyard, are you boy?" boomed the voice of Eight-bellies Eddie, allotment committee member and bodge-and-dodge builder. "He's protecting his kill, you should back off."

Jacob hated Eight-bellies. Hated his big fat beer belly and builder's cleavage. Hated his piggy eyes and the perpetual sneer he had on his chubby face. Hated his criminality. Eight-bellies had learned farming and thieving at an Essex borstal decades ago and had brought both skills to Craggy Farm. Jacob was sure it was Eightbellies who had jemmied his shed door and stolen his rotovator, but had no proof. But now he followed Eight-bellies' advice and retreated slowly.

"Hey Reynard, have some proper scran!" Eight-bellies shouted, throwing down a chicken carcass on the path at the top of Jacob's plot. The fox caught the whiff of roast chicken and scampered to the carcass.

Eight-bellies looked at the fox fondly and then at Jacob and chuckled. "Just like a pet dog, boy. No need to be scared."

"Is he hell a pet dog," Jacob snorted.

"He keeps the rats down. We'd be overrun without him."

"You wouldn't happen to know who moved my scarecrow?"

"No, why would I know that? What do you think I am, boy, a scarecrow minder? Don't even know why you want a bloody scarecrow. Ain't seen that pile of rags scaring nothing. You should have let me burn it when we sorted out Catweazle's effects."

"He works fine for me," Jacob retorted. But immediately regretted the weakness of his response.

Eight-bellies chuckled. "Whatever you say, boy," and strolled off.

The fox followed with the chicken carcass in his mouth.

Jacob watched him go and then said to himself: "One of these days you fat bastard, you'll get what's coming to you. Big time. And I'll be the first to piss on your grave."

Jacob Mortly was a martyr to his piles. That evening one of them prolapsed with thrombosis and strangulation causing Jacob excrutiating pain. He was admitted to hospital and underwent emergency surgery. A week later he felt well enough to return to the allotment and pay a visit to the Tea Club to continue his investigations into who had moved his scarecrow. The Tea Club normally met outside Old Malky's shed on plot 16, but at this time of year they took up winter quarters in the old rusty shipping container down by the back gate.

Legend had it that Eight-bellies Eddie had got the container with the help of Catweazle back in the 1980s. Catweazle had some connection with China and a shipping firm who turned a blind eye to the triads smuggling people into England on their ships. The legend went that this container had arrived at Harwich with 30 dead Chinese illegals, who had suffocated on the voyage, and Eight-bellies had been called in to dispose of the bodies.

Jacob made his way gingerly towards the container, walking cowboy style to avoid chafing his tender bits. Inside, in a warm fug created by a gas cooker and the smoke from roll-ups, sat Old Malky, Bus driver Jim, Geordie Jimmy and Engineer Jim. All folk Jacob was comfortable with. He greeted them. "Alright, Jacob," Engineer Jim said. "Haven't seen you for a few days, have you heard the news?"

"What news? I've been in hospital," Jacob said. Although he didn't want to volunteer why he had been in hospital, he had rehearsed a suitable funny story if pressed.

"It's Eight-bellies Eddie."

"What about him?"

"He's brown bread. Barbara found him on Tuesday at the end of your plot."

"Dead? How? Why?" Jacob said.

"Heart attack," said Engineer Jim.

"Aye," interjected Geordie Jim. "That's what the police told Barbara, but there was something else."

"What?" said Jacob.

"Looks like Old Renyard went for him as he collapsed. Ripped right into his neck and severed his artery." Geordie Jim's face was grave, but his eyes were twinkling.

"You're having me on, right?" Jacob said.

"No, afraid not son," said Old Malky. "There was one hell of a spray of blood. Splashed all over your scarecrow. Distance of what? Two rods?"

The others nodded. "But we did what we could to clean the blood off Black Jake," said Bus driver Jim. "We knows how much you like him."

"That was good of you. So what's going to be done?"

Engineer Jim took a drag on his roll up. "Well we'll wait until after the funeral and then divvy up his stuff. I don't reckon his wife will want anything, she's always said she hates the allotment. And they don't have no kids."

"No, about the fox," Jacob said.

"Oh," Bus driver Jim said, "don't worry about Old Renyard. We've poisoned him. Put Warfarin on some fried chicken. He's gone. We buried him in Eight-bellies' salad bed."

"Aye," said Geordie Jim. "Had to be done. Can't have a rogue fox on the allotment. Even if it means we'll get the rats back."

Eight-bellies Eddie was buried in Chingford Mount cemetery, three rows down from the graves of Ronnie and Reggie Kray. Jacob didn't go to the funeral but did take part in the divvying up of Eightbellies effects and came away with a rusty but working rotavator.

The cold winter gave way to a wet spring and the rats on the allotment went forth and multiplied. By mid June hardly a day went past when Jacob wasn't startled by a young rat shooting out from his compost bin and racing across his plot to burrow under his shed. Such close proximity to rats did nothing to ease Jacob's phobia of the rodents and each time he encountered one, his heart jolted and his muscles were paralysed with fear.

On Midsummer Eve, his cousin Sally de Vie came to visit with her young son Colm. Sally was an English teacher who loved strawberries and Jacob grew the best strawberries on Craggy Farm. After tasting and a picking a basket of strawberries with Colm, Sally took her son's hand and went over to see the scarecrow, walking through its long shadow cast by the afternoon sun. She lifted him Colm up so that he could touch Black Jake's face. Jacob stood at a short distance and smiled with pride.

"See Colm," Sally said. "He's not really that scary is he?"

Colm screwed up his face. "No, he's not scary. He's silly."

Jacob frowned. "Be careful what you say young Colm. Black Jake don't like being called silly."

Colm stuck his tongue out at Jacob. "But he is very silly and stupid."

"I think Colm might need to be taught some manners," Jacob muttered to Sally.

"Oh don't you be a goose, Jacob. He's just being a three-year old."

"You spare the rod, Sally, and you spoil the child. Anyways I must get on, I've got rat traps to set."

"I'll help you," said Sally. "Colm, what would you like to do?"

"I want some of those." Colm said, pointing at Jacob's redcurrants, hanging in strings of shiny red jewels from the bushes near the scarecrow.

"Well why don't you pick some and then come and show them to me," Sally said.

Colm scampered off, allowing Jacob and Sally to make their way to the shed.

"I wouldn't have thought you'd be into setting rat traps," said Jacob.

Sally laughed. "I was brought up in the country as well Jacob. I'm not just a pretty face."

Jacob was relieved that Sally was with him as he didn't like to go near the lairs of the rats on his own.

Sally held a big wooden trap for Jacob as he cut a chunk of old cheese to fit on the balance plate and then pressed the steel spring back to lock it into place. As he was positioning the device in the mouth of a burrow under the shed he was startled by a scream and the trap snapped.

"Bugger!" He said, whipping his fingers back.

"Colm!" Sally shouted, turning from Jacob and sprinting down the plot.

Jacob followed, inspecting his fingers for damage, and found Sally with Colm in her arms. He was sobbing and blood was trickling down his forehead.

"What happened sweetie?" Sally asked gently.

"It was the scarecrow," Colm snuffled. "He scratched me."

Sally looked at Jacob. Jacob shook his head. "He must have scratched his head on the red currant bush. The twigs can be quite sharp," he said. "I've got plasters in the shed. I'll go and get them."

"It was the scarecrow," Colm wailed. "I want to go home!"

As Jacob turned towards the shed he stepped into the shadow of the scarecrow. Something was wrong. He turned back. He had positioned Black Jake so that he always faced north. But now his scarecrow was facing west, towards the shed. How could he have moved? His first thought was Colm. The little herbert had moved him. But how? Black Jake was heavy. Too heavy for a three-year to move. Something was not right. Something was definitely not right.

The day had ended badly. Sally had attacked Jacob for leaving his redcurrant bushes in a dangerous condition and taken a bawling and band-aided Colm home early. The rat traps were still not set and Jacob was not in the mood to attempt the job on his own.

Bollocks, he thought. The longest day deserves a long drink. He went to the local corner shop and brought back 12 cans of Grolsch and a bottle of red wine. He then sat outside his shed and proceeded to drink the cans rapidly. By eight o'clock he was feeling relaxed. By 9 o'clock very happy. Old Malky and Geordie Jimmy walked past the end of his plot on their way home.

"You alright there, Jacob?" Geordie Jimmy shouted.

"Never been better," Jacob replied, lifting his can. "Cheers!"

"Enjoy your drink," said Old Malky raising his hand in farewell. By 9.30pm, Jacob had taken to ruminating. He looked at Black Jake and the shadow spreading out in front of him. Maybe he had got too attached to the scarecrow he thought. Maybe young Colm and Eight-bellies Eddie had a point. What was the point of a scarecrow if it didn't scare birds or children?

"Oi, Black Jake," he slurred. "People think you're stupid. I'm coming to think that you are stupid. You ain't scaring nothing. Not a bloody dicky bird. Tell you what Black Jake…You're fired!"

Jacob giggled at his cleverness and then drained his can. He got to his feet and staggered over to the scarecrow. "Stupid, stupid scarecrow," he said pinching Black Jake's nose. "Tomorrow boy, you burn!"

Jacob made his way back to the shed, his feet unsteadily dancing around the edges of the shadow of the scarecrow. As he did so he was puzzled to see the shadow move as if the scarecrow's arms were lifting. He closed one eye to see if the drink was causing some sort of double vision. The shadow was still moving, the arms stretching out and the fingers on the old gardening gloves on Black Jake's hands elongating.

"I'll be buggered," Jacob said softly. He started to turn but the shadow suddenly swept around him like a cloak. He felt a sharp pain in his neck and an enormous weight on his back – forcing him to the ground. Warm fluid was dripping down his shirt and what felt like teeth were champing into his neck. He screamed and tried to pull himself up from his knees but the weight on his back was too heavy and now something very thin and sharp was tracing its way across his stomach. He looked down and saw a long, shiny, black talon extended from the fingertip of a gardening glove. The talon paused for a second and then sliced into his shirt and into the flesh below. It went deep into his abdomen and then ripped diagonally upwards. Blood seeped out of the narrow incision and Jacob watched with horror as the wound split like the skin on a frying sausage and splayed out causing his intestines to spill out.

"Oh Christ," he moaned. The talon withdrew, dangling a trail of gore. Jacob frantically scrabbled with his hands at the wound trying to push his guts back in but the intestines were too slippery.

Then the weight was suddenly lifted from his back and the teeth removed their grip from his neck. He rolled onto his back and this time was more successful in pushing the coils of intestine back into the wound. Clamping one hand to his belly he raised the other to his neck and caught a powerful spray of blood. His jugular had been cut. He screamed as loud as he could for help. There must be someone still on the allotment, he thought. Someone. Anybody.

A shadow fell on him. He looked up and saw the face of Black Jake, blood dripping from his teeth, his eyes glinting fiery red.

"Oh Jake, I'm sorry. Please stop," he pleaded.

The scarecrow seemed to relent and backed away.

"That's it Jake. No harm done. Me and you are pals. We can patch things up right?" He whispered. Tears filled his eyes. He blinked hard to clear his vision. Black Jake had returned to his old position and the talons had disappeared. It was if he hadn't moved. Jacob began worming backwards along the ground towards the shed, hands still clamped tightly over his wounds. If he could just find some cloth in the shed for bandages, he still had a chance. His mobile was there too. But then he heard the squeals. The squeals of rats. Scenting blood and flesh. His blood and flesh. Jacob's nostrils caught a sharp foul whiff of urine-scented mustiness. He flapped his hands feebly in attempt to frighten the rats away. But it was no good. The lead rat was on him. As he felt its snout bury itself in the gaping wound of his belly and sharp teeth snap onto one his intestines, Jacob Mortley howled.

MAYBE IT'S BECAUSE I'M A LONDONER

WALTHAMSTOW RIOT

L ondon burned and they crapped in my shed
       On my floor at night
They left a big shite
Why they do that, I ain't no Fed?
The main goods on my plot
Are the nice veg for the pot
Does the root of the beet
Have worth on the street?
The allotment brings calm
So why do they harm?
Like the foxes who kill
My pond's frogs for the thrill
These kids want to plunder
And tear all asunder
They shit where they choose
For they have nothing to lose.
Should these urban foxes be shot, or should they be jailed?
Or maybe us adults are the ones who have failed.

PISS MYSELF LAUGHING

First they came for the Jews
    And I chortled at the news
Then the Irish, after a while
And I had to raise a smile
Anti-black humour was a bit near the knuckle
But I still had to chuckle
Targeting the Roma made me laugh out loud
I needed badly to be part of the crowd
Now it's the Muslims who are being given hell
But sorry folks, the jokes are pmsl
Then they came for me and finally I saw
It wasn't a laughing matter
And I didn't laugh no more.

VICTORIA LINE

The folk of Walthamstow
    To work must go
Victoria line at seven twenty
Bringing life a plenty
Like a mighty channel of the Nile
To London all the while.

Once at this hour
Fresh from the shower
Would be the early birds
No exchange of words
Blankness on their face
Staring into space
Or a snoring sleepy head
Dreaming she's still abed.

Now it's packed with masses
Of minimum waged lasses
Cleaners, porters and job mysteries
Bound to the service industries.
Office workers
Office shirkers
School-uniformed teens
Beardy hipsters in jeans.
Afghans, Algerians, and Filipinos
Poles, Lats, maybe even Eskimos
Pretty PAs from Highams Park
Labourers with faces stark.

REASONS TO...

....quit smoking

There was an old man from Torbay
Who smoked 40 fags a day
He coughed day and night
Then lost all his sight
Before painfully passing away.

...stop drinking

There was an old drunk from near Broughty
Whose eyes turned a shade of dark coffee
He rang our Helpline
Saying "I need shome more wine!"
And was told "Sir, we're a charity not an offie."

...eat your greens

Eating spinach, beetroot and curly kale
Won't make you wealthy, but might make you wise
Most important, I can say without fail
It will protect your organs, including your eyes.
And this is not an old wives' tale
Broccoli, cabbage and fresh parsley
As well as keeping you hearty and hale
Will help protect you from the curse of AMD.

MEMO TO CHARITY MANAGEMENT

You've spent oodles on some doodles
 To improve your public looks
But how important is this really
To readers of talking books?

Does your obsession with your brand
Really lend a helping hand?
Will the new logo shade of green
Provide a support on which to lean?

Do you really care a toss
About people with sight loss?
And does my redundancy letter
Really make their lives much better?

BEING THERE

I sensed a womman on the stair
  But when I turned she wasn't there
Another time, I smelt a dog
And only saw a blur in fog
Once I heard the tap of cane
But the sound was faint and not that plain
I walked down feeling bolder
Then a hand touched my shoulder
And I heard a softy voice
Saying:"You are here out of choice
I am not and my life is stark
I needed help to escape the dark
I needed people to innovate
But you left it far too late
I needed people who really care
I needed people to be there."

THE POWER OF FIRE

Burn bonfire burn
Dark spirits I thee spurn
Oh cursed black dog
Choke on my blazing log
To the monkey on my back
Take a jump into my stack
Begone you evil winter sprites
Flee in terror from my flames and lights.

THE LAST OF WINTER

Still winter has not released its icy grip
On the sleeping soil of my allotment strip
I pick cabbage and sage for the pot
So all is not dead in my plot
Gold narcissi and purple croci
Push their flowers to the sky
Vibrant in the glistening frost
The cold damp darkness surely lost.

11349093R00050

Printed in Great Britain
by Amazon.co.uk, Ltd.,
Marston Gate.